THOSE HIDDEN OBSTRUCTIONS

MICHAEL BETANCOURT

WILDSIDE PRESS

Published by Wildside Press LLC.
www.wildsidepress.com

CONTENTS

DEAD, BY DAWN

My brother shoved the pack at me while tying it to my belt, pushing hard, making my underwire bra cut into me. He was moving so fast I didn't have time to think. "You're going to need this stuff," he said, taking item after item off the gurney and putting them into the main pocket: candles, matches, packets of cigarettes (and he calls himself a doctor?) but when he was going to put the packet of paper money in the bag, I had to say something. That was probably good since there was no way this was a good idea. Grief makes you crazy.

"*Hell* money? You're kidding, right?"

He pulled the zipper closed. "Not at all. You have no idea what you're going to run into, and several million dollars may be just what you need."

Doug continued his preparations, paying no attention to my lack of belief. This whole plan was madness. How did I let him talk me into it? But I knew why. Rob was lying somewhere cold, and I wanted him back. I could feel the tears trying to start, again. "Just were do you think I'm going?"

"Lie back and unbutton your shirt. I need to get the heart monitor hooked up and get the IV in."

I followed my doctor's instructions. "Pervert." He ignored me. He already had me out of my jeans. The exam table had that weird plastic warmth that squeaks under your butt.

"Ok. While I'm getting you set up, run through it again. What happens when you're on the beach?" He stuck the foam patches to my chest.

"Hey! Those are cold."

"The beach. You'll be there only for a minute or two before you get sent back. Run through it. If you screw this up, I don't know if we'll be able to get a second shot. At least not while you're alive."

I nodded. "Fine. When I get to the beach, I run for the water, not towards the trees. When I get there, I should look for the dock and take a boat across."

The monitor chirped loudly once, then started buzzing. Doug cursed softly, and pushed the reset button. "I hate this one, temperamental, but so does the nursing staff. Nobody'll notice it's gone." He stared at the readouts. "Ok. Good. Now lie back. Don't forget the rules I told you.

They'll get you through, sis."

Suddenly the exam room felt small and cold, and I felt foolish lying on the table, wired up, IV in my arm. This wasn't going to work. Rob was gone and I want him back. It was a stupid idea that would never work because it was crazy. I wanted him back so much I'd do something stupid. The tears started. But Doug was too busy to notice: buzzing back and forth between counter and storage cubbies, laying out his tools. I felt like he must be humoring me and my crazy idea about getting Rob back. Visit the land of the dead? Yeah, right. That's just dumb. But there Doug was, getting everything ready. Humoring me.

Then suddenly he stopped. "Shit. I almost forgot. You're going to need these most of all." He dug in his pocket and pulled out a tiny manila envelope. "I've got six gold coins here. You'll need two to get across the river, and then for your return you'll need four more—two for you and two for Rob." He came over, pushing them into my jeans pocket and tossing me my pants. "You should put these on again. And your shoes." He turned back to his preparations, still not very busy.

I did as he said. "Ok. Anything else?" Now I knew he was just humoring me.

There was a pause, hand in pocket. "I know you're going to think this is even dumber than the hell money, but I want you to take my iPhone with you too."

"I don't think I'm going to be making any calls where I'm going."

He laughed. It was surprising, joyful and unexpected. "No. I have a playlist of lullabies on here that we use on long trips to help Lily sleep. It might come in handy, I don't know. Besides, it's not like I won't be getting it back. I'm not so sure about the gold coins." He frowned, his voice trailing off. "Gold's different, somehow."

"What do you mean by gold's different? Have you done this before?" Now, the fear was back. He was really going to do it? Kill his grief stricken sister? The idea that this might be malpractice jumped into my head, and suddenly I was afraid. Why did he agree to this?

He ignored me, and I was out of time. "I think we're ready. You'll feel a spike of cold, then you should be on the beach. Don't forget the stuff we went over. Remember, I don't think we can do this twice, at least not anytime soon."

"Have you?" I nodded, leaning back, giving in, feeling the weight of the bag on my chest, the snug fit of my jeans, the little pinch where my bra closes in back, the tightness of my shoelaces. I guess I'm not going to get an answer. I knew he'd look worried if I looked over at him, so I didn't. I was still crying, but I didn't know if it was for Rob or myself. "Ready."

As Doug pushed down and the cold ran up my arm, I'm positive the last thing I heard was him humming "Happy Trails." Perverse bastard. All I could think was I hope this works, and I was standing in the deep dark of night. I could feel more than see that I wasn't alone. It was confusing: where was I? As my eyes adjusted to the darkness, I realized it was a beach, *the beach.* The one Rob had told me about. I stood there for a moment, wondering if it was a dream, or just a hallucination. To the right, in the distance, were fluffy black shapes of trees, dark shadows of people stood around, close, but not too close. Just like Rob had said. The soft sand slid around my feet. It was quiet and calm, I felt tense. How did I let him talk me into this? Oh yeah, it was my idea.

I was on the beach: *Run!*

I did.

*

Running on packed sand is easy; wet sand can be treacherous, but loose, soft sand is almost impossible. It slides away, and for all the exertion, you don't get very far—but I kept running anyway and didn't stop until I got to the water. The silence was deafening.   Like everything else, it was black and almost invisible in the darkness. The amorphous shapes—land?—sky?—trees?—filled the distance and I knew there were other people on the beach with me even though I didn't know where they were. My feet in the sand didn't make slapping noises. There was no familiar hiss of the sand moving as a ran. Sound had an unfamiliar quality, like it was a foreign, unwelcome visitor keeping its distance.

I paused at the water's edge of what I knew was a river. But if I hadn't already known that, I might have thought it was a lake or sea because of the way the shore curved around it. I was either standing in a small bay or at some bend where the opposite shore lay hidden, too far to see across. The idea that I was now just outside the land of the dead was silly. I walked along the shore. Rob was gone, and I could feel the tears running again, slow and hot on my face. I can't get him back, that's not how the world works. It occurred to me that Doug must have given me some weird drug and was now letting me sleep it off, so I might was well go with it. Maybe if I dream about seeing Rob, it'll make it feel better. I brushed the tears back. Better to stay focused.

Now what? Doug had said look for the dock, but there wasn't anything to see: just river and sandy shore. Nothing grew along the edges of the water, just sand fading into smooth black waters. From the distance behind me I could hear whooping. I dropped to the ground, leaning up to try and see over the dune, but there was nothing. And as suddenly as it started, silence returned. I waited a moment, but the sounds didn't return, so I got up again, climbing back to the top of the dune. All was stillness, silence and dark.

I thought maybe I'd be able to see the dock better from up there, and I was right—in the distance, maybe a mile or two away up the shore was a tiny light. It hung low over the water, faint like a star, but definitely not in the sky. It was a sign of something, and since there weren't any other options, I headed for it, thinking about how each step was a step closer to finding Rob, to getting him back.

There didn't seem to be any need to run, so I just focused on getting there, trudging along in the loose sand until I reached the light. Funny thing is,

I got the feeling it met me half way, even though that seems impossible. And there I was, and the dock was so much less than I expected. Only ten feet long, it stretched from the sand out just barely into the water. A series of words presented themselves to describe it: un-impressive, un-satisfying, un-safe. They all started with un- and even then fell short of how little there was to this dock.

The light was something else, though. And as I got closer to it, I realized it was hung over the dock on a chain stretching taut directly up into the sky. At the end of the chain was a reflector and a honeycomb cage holding the light, directing what little illumination it gave off down onto the dark boards of the dock. The lamp just hung there, apparently attached to nothing. Just dock and weird lantern.

I must have climbed down and gone out onto the dock without thinking about it, staring up at the light. I guess this is what moths feel battering themselves against street lamps, drawn to the light. The tiny spark was hypnotizing. Who knows how long I stood there dumbly staring up at it, unable to figure out what it was attached to or where the light was really coming from—there was no bulb, or wick, or any other source for the light. There was just light shining down from inside the honeycomb cage.

The boatman may have been waiting patiently for hours, or could have just arrived when I noticed him standing at the edge of the dock. Completely wrapped in black cloth—shrouded, I guess—he towered over his tiny boat. Silent, like everything else, he was simply waiting for me to notice his presence. That fact scared me. Would he have waited forever? Is this what they mean by "patience of the dead?" Was this really happening?

I felt like I should apologize. "Sorry. I didn't see you there." I walked over to him. "Is this your boat?" *Dumb question. Of course it's his boat. He's a boatman, that's his boat.* I felt foolish for asking. Once I got closer and could see him better in the light I realized there wasn't anything to see, just the wrapping, coarse cloth bound around something else that I couldn't see. Somehow he had managed to stand in my shadow, as if hiding from the lantern's glow. As I got closer—had the dock grown larger while I looked at the light?—I suddenly needed to explain myself to him.

"Um. I'm looking for my husband. I think he's already here, somewhere. My brother Doug says you can take me to him." I tried to look him in the eye, but even with the aid of the lamp hanging over the dock, there was nothing to see but shadows.

He, or maybe I should be saying it, stuck out a paw. It was a funny little thing, like the little hands my hamster had when I was a child. Suggestions of fingers, long and boney, but not human. Not at all. I stared at it, not sure what to do. Then I remembered the envelopes. "Just a moment. I think I have what you need. I'm supposed to pay in gold, right?" I felt for them, and there they were, where Doug had stuck them. It seemed a lifetime ago I'd had that conversation. Pulling one out I set it on the boatman's paw.

"There you go."

I'm not sure what I expected. It to take the packet, rip it open with its hamster teeth and chew on the little gold coins inside like they were filled with chocolate, maybe. But it didn't happen. Maybe I expected an answer, a word. The packet just sat there and we looked at each other. I took the packet back. *Fool. How am I ever going to find Rob if I can't even do this right?*

"Sorry. New to all this." I laughed. It was an uncertain giggle, quiet, disappearing into the darkness. The boatman didn't respond and I was getting tense, if I screwed this up, would I just be stuck here along the river bank, unable to go anywhere? Rob was out there, I knew it. "I do have the fare. Just let me get it out of this for you." Tearing the envelope open carefully, so not to lose the tiny coins, I shook one out into its open paw.

The boatman moved quickly, but without any sound, and was back on the boat, pushing the prow towards the dock. I climbed carefully inside. I felt excited, happy—he was taking me to find Rob—this crazy idea was going to work.

The boat looked like a combination of a Viking ship and a gondola, but without any grace: hacked wood coarsely fit together, I wondered how it could stay afloat. It was the kind of thing a child might make from bits of trash and discarded lumber, assembling them without any real understanding of how boats actually work. *That you need to keep the water out.* Yet it didn't sink when I got in and sat down in the prow. It was really happening. Doug hadn't just humored me, and for the first time, I knew it wasn't a dumb idea or some silly fantasy. I was going to go get him and we'd go home again and be together. It was really going to be that simple. I was going to bring Rob back with me. I smiled at the boat, the river, anything that would notice.

The boatman punted away from the dock and

we moved out into the current, slow and smoothly flowing—taking us downstream and across to the far shore.

The spark of the lamp abruptly went out, dropping everything into sea of black where there wasn't even the sound of water splashing. For the first time I was really scared as the dark pressed in and I could see nothing. *Was the boat really there?* There was nothing to see, and even less to feel. There was no way to be sure I was still in the boat and suddenly I knew there was something wrong. I couldn't hear any of the little noises you take for granted. Your breath, the soft hiss of clothing, the minor pains and tiny senses that tell you you're alive. Just the darkness and silence, pressing in and down around me. I realized that I was dead. Really dead, not the playing dead, or make believe that happens in dreams. I felt myself cursing Doug for letting me, helping me do this. It was a bad idea. It wasn't going to work. It hadn't worked. Rob was gone and I couldn't even feel the tears I knew I was crying. This was a trick, a trap, there was nothing more. Just the darkness, the endless black.

I tried counting to pass the time, I don't know how far I got. A million? Two? And the darkness continued, the endless silence, without feeling.

Without thinking about it memories came forward, all those little petty things. The mean things they said about my hair in third grade. The taunting about not having the right jeans. All the times I would bring something to school only to have it broken, or stolen. My memories didn't keep the silence and the empty black at bay, but they kept coming. The panic at having to stand up and give my book report and stuttering through the title while the class laughed. The party where I got drunk and the next day Jackie called me a slut. And the darkness continued pressing in. *Why did I tell Doug my idea? What was I thinking?* It was a mistake, Rob was gone now I would never find him. All that was left were my memories, trying to fill the emptiness, the dark. And there were so few of them. The awkward moment in the back of the car when my boyfriend pulled his pants down and looked at me. Waiting outside the office and seeing Rob coming down the steps. The bee flying around Rob's ear, and him swatting at it, unaware what it was. Standing next to the hospital bed looking at Rob, feeling the cold hard metal. His still body, lifeless as the doctor paused at the door. I wanted to cry, but they came and were gone, and the darkness remained, smothering me, pressing down, around filling everything with void and it would never end. This was a mistake. I should not have done this. *What was I thinking?*

If I opened my mouth to scream, I knew no sound would come out. There was nothing I could do now. I was dead, but I wanted to be with Rob again. I had failed. It didn't work, it was a mistake to think I could do something, a dumb fantasy. I was dead, and this is what death was like. No sensation, not even my hands pressing together. Just this emptiness forever and me trapped in it, straining for anything, however tiny to remind me that I was there, that I wasn't all alone, hoping, grasping against that void. And there was nothing.

*

The journey lasted hours or days or years, there was no way to tell. Abruptly we were at another dock, larger, more of a pier, well lit by lamps bending down from tall posts running along the center. It was just there, and suddenly the crossing was over, and I was standing at the far end staring down towards shore. It was strange. The boat pulled in close, I stood up and stepped off quickly, wanting nothing more to do with the abyss I had just passed through, and the boatman was gone. I didn't miss him or his hellish boat as

I tried not to think about the return journey.

The silence and darkness still pressed in, but the light, faint filling the dock with midnight pools was like honey and the crossing quickly seemed like a bad memory of a pain that is gone without explanation or reason. I hadn't moved an inch since getting off the boat and it didn't matter. I wasn't trapped in the blackness any more, I had made it across. I could just stand there on the pier and everything was going to be okay simply because the choking darkness was gone and I could, would find Rob in this place. About halfway down, I could see several piles of crates, bunched up around several of the lights. I started walking towards them, wondering if he was waiting for me there.

They filled the pier, leaving only a narrow path through. Large crates and smaller crates, they sat in disorderly heaps, clearly having been left at different times, and arranged carefully to make a web, but never so high as to make the passage completely dark. Looking at the crates as I passed, I could see no writing on them, or marks of any kind. I got the feeling they had been dropped off and then abandoned, I guess whatever they held no longer mattered. I had just passed the end of the piles, about half way to the shore, when I heard a voice yell, "You finally came! It's about time."

I spun around, looking to see whose it was. A man wearing a tattered suit that had fit at one time, but now hung loose was getting up from sitting against a bunch of crates behind me. "I've been waiting here for ages. Took you long enough!" His voice was cracked, a raspy, harsh sound. Nothing like Rob's. I didn't know him.

"Who are you?"

"Don't give me that. You know who I am. I've been waiting, Matilda. I told you not to keep me waiting." His right arm was balling into a fist, and he took a stiff-armed swing at me as he came closer, but missed since I was still out of reach. "You know better than to keep me waiting. Wasting my time here." I could see his face, now. Old, dried up looking, and creased by too much anger to too long. "I have to do everything."

I backed away, glancing towards the shore. "My name's not Matilda." I took a few steps away as he staggered forward, swinging again and missing.

"You're always taking, taking, taking. I hate doing this. You should be happy that I waited for you." He ran forward grabbing my pack, a swinging his other arm toward my head. "How could you do this to me? Making me wait for you?" His blow had no weight behind it. More like being slapped by a pillow. I shoved him back, pulling free of his grasp. I could see his face curled into a snarl.

"I'm *not* Matilda. Leave me alone!" I pushed him, watching his knees fold, as he fell backwards. "I bet she came through here a long time ago and got away from you." I ran for the shore, glancing back to see him sitting on his ass, watching me go. How many other people had he attacked? Now I knew why the dock was full of crates. This jerk must've been attacking everyone who arrived. I wondered how Rob had dealt with him. He'd always been good at calming people down, making peace. I think that was what first attracted me to him—he felt safe.

I had reached the end of the pier where a much darker staircase went raggedly up the hillside. Vacant houses leaned over the top, and terrace walls filled with debris stretched out to either side as I climbed up. Somewhere in the middle I found myself counting, in rhythm to my footsteps. I reached the top, and turned around to see where I'd been. Vertigo swung at me, and I grabbed a wall for support. I was hundreds of feet up, at the top of an almost vertical incline. The stairs hadn't looked as steep from below. The pier was a bright strip, half filled with dark crates. The violent guy had disappeared. I guessed he was hiding somewhere in the piles of crates. *What a shithead. No wonder he hasn't met Matilda here.*

I turned back from the dizzying view. A paved road stretched out in front of me, more of the vacant buildings on either side. Built from stone, and with barred or shuttered windows, they lined the road. There was no where to go but forward. I was alone.

The empty houses, their faces ashen in the darkness were built right up to the road, they stood over me while I walked down the center of the street, glancing at their vacancy in passing. Shuttered windows and closed doors greeted me. What sort of a place was this? I had the feeling they were watching me, but it was a vacant town, one long abandoned, like a summer vacation town in winter, the residents long since packed up to go home, leaving their houses empty, closed up for a long slumber as I passed by them block after block of silent facades, closed doors and hidden windows. I saw no one, and began to wonder if the only other person in this whole place was the angry man down by the water, waiting forever on the dock.

My thoughts drifted black to Rob. Had he passed through here, or had he been caught by the angry man on the dock, and held there against his will inside one of the many coxes and crates that lay piled. The vacancy of the town made me doubt that he had passed through and I was starting to think of returning, retracing my way when I could hear sounds of laughter and talking from just up ahead.

Without warning the street turned a corner and opened into a large square filled almost of overflowing with picnic tables and chairs. As I came closer to the turn the voices grew louder, stopping only as I stepped around the bend and could see what lay beyond. Somehow my presence must have interrupted the party since as I drew close enough to see into the grand square with its tables filled with food and drink, the voices stopped and all that remained were the empty chairs. The plates, food and drinks left in place for a party of none, the guests having left the remains for someone else to clean up. I stood looking at the zigzag mess of tables and chairs, and realized how hungry I was, how very long it had been since I last ate, and how good the piles of grilled chicken, roasted corn, and steaming piles of everything smelled like I should just pull up a chair and make myself at home.

I didn't.

Going carefully through the tangle I gradually crossed the square, being careful not to sit down, not taste the food I knew would be the most delicious thing I would ever try, the last meal I would ever have. My brother's warning echoing with each step as I passed by the chocolate mousse, the raspberry tart, the bar-be-que and roast, the candied and glazed food, and decorated table after table each smelling and looking better than the last—do not eat anything while you are there—I had come to find Rob and nothing could stop me reaching him. Not pizza or chocolate or any of the other guilty pleasures piled on the tables just within reach.

And I came to the end of town, a sudden end, the houses leaning on each other and then, empty landscape, the road continuing in a straight line. Short trees and tall cypress lined the roads shoulders, replacing the regular line of houses against the dark sky with jagged stabs into the darkness. Distant echoes of bird calls, like a nightingale, drifted down to the road from somewhere. I continued down the road, keeping close to the side in case there might be traffic— even though I doubted there would be any. I was wrong.

A parked car, drawn off and left at the side of the road gradually seemed to rise up as I climbed a low hill. Down the other side and beyond it, the road turned left slightly and one side opened to the void, letting me look over the river far below. Dark waters were gliding past a sheer face of rock in silence. There was nothing else to see: no distant shore waiting beyond the surging waters. I turned back to the road and kept walking, each step a hope that I was drawing closer to Rob, knowing that I must be since there was no where else to go.

The road turned inland, moving away from the cliff and slowing winding downhill to a fork in the road, with a parasol and a recliner where I could see someone look up as I came closer, watching my approach. At first I thought it was Rob, but as I walked closer, I knew it couldn't be. "Hello. I doubt you know who I'm looking for, but maybe you can help me anyway?"

The man looked up at me from his lawn chair and said "Ah ha! I am the Devil, the prince of lies, to answer my riddle, look deep into my eyes. I know which way your love has gone, so ask your question, lest you choose wrong." He spread his hands, gesturing towards the right and left, the roads stretching off from where he sat.

I tried not to giggle. He was dressed in a tweed cape and looked exactly like Jeremy Brett, the actor who played Sherlock Holmes on TV. I looked at him carefully. If this was the Devil, I was going to have trouble taking anything he said seriously. But I figured I should play along anyway, just in case. "My question? You mean which way to go?" He nodded, once, curtly, like it was obvious and beneath him to answer.

So I asked my question, then went the opposite way.

Rob was nearby. The road leveled out and passed through a covered bridge over a tiny stream rolling and bouncing over rocks. It was picturesque: overhanging trees, clumps of reeds and bamboo, a boulder. On the far side I could see small clusters of people walking in circles together, their heads nodding in conversations I could only guess at as I crossed, my pace slowing as I searched faces for the one I recognized. Rob was here! I smiled so happy to see him, feeling tears running down my cheek my face grew hot. He was here! I made it, everything could be alright. Relief. I wanted to run and discovered I already was.

"Rob, I've been looking for you everywhere

here, you don't have to stay!" I wanted to get his attention, he didn't seem to recognize me. As I got closer, I could see the dark welt on his neck, the bee sting.

He looked through me.

I grabbed his arm, pulling at him. "Rob? Don't you know me?" It was so quiet, I could feel my words echoing back softly.

"Come on, Rob!" I leaned up and gave him a little kiss.

His eyes focused on me. "What are you doing here?"

Relief! He knew me, it was going to be okay. "I'm here to get you, you can come with me!" I pulled at his hand, hanging limp by his side.

"Why would I go with you? You did this to me. It's your fault. You put me here." He pulled his hand back with a jerk. "You killed me."

"No . . ." It was a mistake.

"All I asked you to do was carry my *Epipen* in your purse, was that too much to ask? You did this to me, why would I want to be with you?"

"I'm sorry."

"This is all your fault. You killed me."

"No, Rob. It's a mistake." He was so angry. "No, I . . ."

"Yeah my mistake, I should never have trusted

you. It's your fault I'm here, Dawn. You killed me and now I'm here. Go away." He slapped at me, a wild, flinging gesture, "I'm dead now, and it's your fault. You put me here."

"But you don't have to stay, I came to get you."

He laughed, a hollow, ringing sound. "Yeah, right." And he turned and walked way.

My throat was tight. There was nothing more to say as he walked away down the road, his head shaking back and forth with each step farther away from me.

And I headed back, over the bridge and down the road to the dock, crossing back through the terrible dark to the beach. As Doug had said, I was sent back, waking into the pain of living. He took me home and put me in the spare room to rest peacefully. After a few hours of poor sleep I lay looking at the night stand, a glass of water standing there as testimony to someone checking on me. Lily must have come too: a pink dinosaur lay in the doorway. I could hear cartoon voices and her laughter, faintly, from downstairs. Everything ached.

I sat up and pulled myself over to the dresser where I'd dumped the stuff from my pockets and dropped my belt. Crumpled papers and wadded up tissues made a little mound. A printed card with "I sent my soul through the invisible, some letter of that afterlife to spell: and by and by my soul returned to me and answered, 'I myself am Heaven and Hell.' — Omar Khayyám, *The Rubaiyat of Omar Khayyám"* on it caught my eye for a moment and I paused.

I felt my nose dripping. Fishing around in the mess quickly for a clean tissue, I accidentally knocked my belt off the edge, sending it snaking towards the floor, taking the pile of trash with it.

Two of Doug's envelopes fluttered away, empty, while the third bounced downwards with a clink. He'd said gold was different. I wondered at it for a moment, then remembered how thorough my brother was. *Whatever.* I blew my nose.

I had a funeral to arrange.

TIDE OF SONG

The door opened and Jacob stood behind it, dressed in a creaseless white suit, a light gray-on-gray cravat tied carefully, the pattern too subtle to notice, it would shift strangely under a direct gaze. A quick look at his watch, and, "Right on time. Glad you could come. None of the others have arrived, yet."

He led the way through a large house with many rooms, some open, others closed, until we arrived at an octagonal solarium, with mirrored walls reflecting the grassy lawn stretching behind the house; the haze of London fogged the distance. He walked past the furniture half-facing the windows to pick up a glass from under a lily-pond lamp, surrounded on three sides by the sofas. I've known him for several years, but it was the first time I'd visited his house.

I didn't know how to react.

"I collect." Turning as he went to the bar: "Would you like a drink? Not everything was acquired by me; my wife chose many of the Nouveau pieces.

This was one of her favorites. What would you like?" The doorbell rang faintly.

"Um . . . whatever." He handed me the glass, then left to answer the bell. I looked out the window. In the distance statues rose from behind a hedge and a sparrow hopped across the grass.

Jacob returned, interrupting my thoughts by introducing the two people who followed. A tall, but mousy man and an equally tall, fat woman. "Mark Magruder, this is Natasha Tyler and John Ingram." Both looked like escapees from 1900. I guessed they were the pair from the Royal Academy of Arts Jacob talked about off and on.

We shook hands, and they sat opposite me. Natasha wore a long red taffeta dress and John had on the steel rimmed glasses so popular then, while Jacob poured drinks.

"Are you expecting anyone else?"

Jacob looked up, his reflection addressing me, "Yes, she will arrive soon and meet us in the study. No need to hurry, we have time." He seated himself on the third sofa. "Mark is an antique dealer. I believe that is what you are calling yourself, am I correct?"

I nodded; he continued. "Of course, that is not quite true. He also collects: only the more unusual pieces, I believe. If you ever decide to part with those glass pieces, I will never forgive you if you don't tell me first."

"Fine." I smiled, then said, "What I collect I seldom sell. The selling part is more from necessity than desire. I became a dealer to get rid of the pieces I didn't want. You often get several pieces at an auction, when you only want one out of the lot—a necessity. Auctions are like that."

Natasha nodded; John played with a hangnail. "Time to go, just bring the glasses along." Jacob led the way down a different hall, past small framed paintings.

We came to the study, and a woman wearing a green evening dress stood at a bookshelf, reading. When we entered, she turned, brushing shoulder-length blond hair out of her face. "Hello Mark, Natasha, John. Father, what took you so long?"

"I don't believe we've met," I said, setting the glass on a table, "but you seem to know me."

"Actually we have met, but it was two years ago at your New Year's Eve party. I went with my father, but left early."

"I still don't remember you."

Smiling, "Oh well, don't worry about it." She opened a set of sliding doors in the corner, "Dinner's waiting."

Jacob crossed the room; we followed. The

dining room had a southerly view, out across the carefully trimmed yard to a stand of cypress trees. Inside the bay windows, a table held various covered dishes. A crystal chandelier filled the room with light; the setting sun had filled the yard with a golden-red brilliance.

We sat. Jacob poured the wine while a servant came in and served. We ate in silence, knives chirping on porcelain. Finally: "This party is to celebrate my success. I admit that it sounds very self serving and egocentric, nonetheless, what we are all celebrating is the completion of a project I have been working on for the past year. It is an investment, of sorts. And it promises to have great returns for the funds taken up. I will not bore you with the details; be assured it is a large amount."

I looked around the table—Natasha frowning, John unreadable, Vicki smiling—at least I wasn't the only one who'd been left out. "What's this project?"

"Did I not say? Very well then; it can wait until you have met Maro. It will be much clearer then." Jacob drank the rest of his wine in a mouthful. Suddenly he was standing, "Come," and led the way back down the hall, pausing to unlock a door with a key on a ring attached to his pants.

Beyond were cracked plaster walls, a bare

lightbulb, a set of stairs descending into blackness. "Wait, I will turn the lights on." He vanished into the darkness.

A minute later we followed, a weak yellow light had gone on. I was at the back of the group that went down. Bare walls, metal shelving and boxes were at the periphery, in a corner was a 1950s-vintage bomb shelter complete with locked door.

In the center of the floor, resting on an apron of ragged-edged gray carpet stood the instrument, the chromed steel and smooth lusterless black plastic parts all turned golden under the warm yellow light. Jacob ran his fingers along it, tracking the flow of light. Vicki moved at the edge of my vision, unpacking a spool of silvery tape and loading it into a recorder of some sort. When she finished, she nodded at Jacob.

"Have a seat, chairs are right there. No! In the corner.'

"What's this thing?" Natasha asked.

"All will be revealed."

Waiting, I unfolded a chair and sat at the base of the stairs. Above, the door finished its slow swing closed with a thud-click. No one else noticed.

The canvas chair was not comfortable. *Wonder when he'll get to the point.* Looking at the instrument, my eyes running over the graceful drape of wires, a cascade of cables connecting the many parts. The shadows played tricks with the light, weaving it together into a confusing tangle.

"Beautiful, no?" The light highlighted the smoothness of the chrome, vanished into the darkness of the recesses, danced along the smooth flow of colored wires, gold tipped leads and silvery connections. We nodded our agreement. It was a piece of finely crafted sculpture, resting alone, dominating the space gently. It was beautiful.

"But what does it do?" John.

Jacob pressed a red switch, and—

"A musical instrument, completely unique, unlike any other. The music it will produce is completely new, original, and more beautifully complex than any which has been before. It cost a fortune; it will make me ten times as many."

—and the speakers hummed to life, then quieted.

From a box on the metal shelving, Jacob removed a black plastic box; he removed and loaded a tranquilizer gun. "Vicki would you unlock the door please?" Jacob stepped over to it, swung the door wide and fired. The only sound was the faint hum of the speakers, and the sound of a body falling onto concrete, softly visceral, unpleasant.

We stared in shocked silence.

"John, Mark, would you please help me with him?"

I was too shocked and horrified to rise. John wasn't , he helped carry the limp body of a man in his middle twenties over to the instrument. "Thank you."

Jacob strapped the limp form into a chair, pulling a metal box over the head. Screws held it in place. Gold sockets ringed the top, and open slots ran down the front of the face. The mess of wires connected to the helmet and lay across the heaving chest. Softly, Maro's breathing rasped against the helmet.

"Can he breathe in that?" Natasha.

"Vicki, the lights, if you would?" Darkness crashed down, only split by the faint glow of tiny lights on the instrument. But only for a short time, soon a different glow would fill the room.

In the darkness, Jacob spoke quietly, "I have long been interested in the power of music, in what scholars once called 'The Music of The Spheres,' once believed in, but no more. I, however, know better. That music, which those scholars heard, does exist; it is real. In a moment, you will hear what no man has heard for centuries."

Very theatrical, I thought as Jacob allowed time for his words to echo in the silence. At the end of it, he turned his machine on.

I didn't notice any change in the atmosphere at first, it was so slight. Then, it happened.

As sudden as the dawn, the room was filled with a faint, clear greenish glow, as if the room were filled by millions of fireflies, or glowing watch faces. It was a clear, magical glow, beautiful: the glow seen in bogs and swamps, the light of the wil'o'wisp. The light of things dying in southern seas. The glow of things rotting, the phosfluorescent glow of death, itself.

As the glow grew in brightness, much of it seemed to settle around the still, black form of a man I never met, the person called Maro, was starting to glow like a coal.

Then two things happened at once: Maro screamed and the music began.

*

There were no instruments, only sliding, fleeting notes out of harmony with each other, but producing an odd holistic unity. Maro screamed again, and was silent. The music continued, strong, lonely, each of several melodies rising like waters, a wind drifting across the surface of a sea, while darker forces rose from the depths. With the wind came the first hints of a storm. In the skies above, the stars swirled, a brilliant band of light that divided the night, looming brilliantly while comets and shooting stars swung in an insane dance with the swirling waters that crashed onto the red and gray rocks below me.

The land was still, only the grass swaying to the wind as smaller animals chased one another toward a gate guarded by a red crab and lobster, their claws locked in a macabre embrace.

Their dance continued beneath the howling wind which made the grasses dance and the stones of the wall quiver. Blowing leaves of autumn passed in front of me, obscuring their dance. I rose to see better, the wind swirled around them, around me, playfully plucking at my clothes, pulling me forward, carrying me deeper into the music, the warbling melodies colliding around me as the leaves swirled, dancing across the stones of the path that lay at my feet. The wind swayed

around me, a light breeze, forcing movement forward, tugging at me, begging my indulgence.

A dancing dog came toward me, growing large too quickly for the distance covered. I followed him as he danced away from me toward a stand of trees nestled between two hills. The sky suddenly lit with a blaze of light bursting forth and moving down onto the ground to form an ocean stirred by strange, dark currents. As the waters approached my feet, I hurried up the nearby hill, the dog having danced away.

A storm began to rise across the waters, bringing each wave of light to crash down onto me. It was as if I had drunk some magical elixir with strange powers that had caused my exile from the world I knew.

The moon began to swing in a strange dance as the heavens, once more, began their spiral. Dizzy, I fell down, lying on the ground, watching the grasses swirl around me; they danced like tiny people at a ball, dancing a minuet, exquisite clothes moving in spirals and flourishes. The violence of their dance surprised me: how could the tiny people perform a dance while swinging at each other with swords that draped and flowed more like leaves of grass than foils of steel?

Continuing to gyrate, the heavens looked down

onto me with pleasant eyes, passed a transparent hand over me. Winds rose up carrying me away, a dust mote in the sky. I rose up and fell back again, into a sea of light, moved only by the tides of song.

I felt the spiraling sea begin to quiet, the strength of the song begin to pass, leaving me lying on gray, smooth stone. I lay on my face, breathing the cool, dry dust that had collected at some time in the past. I opened my eyes to see the yellowish warm light, heralding a dawn. The last of the breezes brushed past me gently, softly, rustling down through the dust on the floor in a tiny dust devil.

Pushing down, I rose from the floor and wobbly grabbed the back of my chair. The room was silent, the song at an end. I looked toward the instrument; Jacob stood beside it grinning, his white teeth wetly reflecting the light. The chair where Maro lay strapped was empty.

Natasha, John and Vicki were also absent.

"What?" Rough, my voice sounded like I was dying of thirst.

"Just a moment," Jacob turned from pouring me a drink from a bottle that rested on a shelf, formerly vacant. My hands had trouble holding onto the square of cut crystal. I sniffed the light red liquor: sherry. "Quite dry." Jacob toasted me with his glass.

I sipped; nodded.

"We were worried when you were missing at the end of the performance. I think Maro is getting better at playing it. Practice you know." Jacob paused. "I am sorry if I scared you before he performed; these neurosensors are very sensitive, so he must prepare himself as best he can under these somewhat limited conditions.

"I assure you he is quite all right."

I tried my strangely tired voice again. "What happened? I don't understand."

"Neither do we. When the lights came on, you were gone. Vicki and the others, they are off looking for you. John suggested that, perhaps, you had tired and left. I chose to wait down here to see if you wandered in. You did not."

"What, then?"

"About a minute ago, you suddenly appeared on the floor, stood up and sat where you are now. I do not understand it."

"I'm not sure what happened, one minute I'm sitting here, listening, and the next, well, it's as if the music carried me off. I do remember waves and wind."

"Interesting. Can you continue? I would like

to get a recording of this, it is strange, you must agree. Come upstairs, I will get Vicki's attention on the intercom."

I turned and headed upstairs, followed by his footsteps. The lights clicked off; darkness returned.

Jacob led me back to his study. I didn't see him call Vicki, but a moment later she appeared ("Natasha and John had to go home. It's a long drive.") carrying a large tape recorder and a pair of microphones which she sat on a table, pulling Queen Anne chairs over to it. I sat in one, she in the other.

While she fiddled with the contraption, adjusting recording levels, she said. I stared at the intricately carved claw holding a wooden ball that greatly resembled a globe, the continents all contorted: Europe was larger than Asia.

Finally Vicki signaled her readiness.

I should never have told them what happened. But I did and that is what damns me: I repeated my story, with more detail. When I finished, I stifled a yawn, and Jacob suggested I stay the night in one of the second-floor guest bedrooms.

I agreed; the view from my window was of the line of cypress trees, their black forms standing out against the brightness of the night sky. The moon was almost full.

Faint music came drifting to my ears, from under the door, through the cracks; only Mozart, *not the song*. Turning from the window, I lay on the bed, gentle notes drifting through the air, moonlight drifting through the windows. And I slept, not to be disturbed by dreams.

*

Blindingly bright light woke me, when the white haze cleared, Jacob sat in a chair. I could smell him across the room, something had happened. I got out of bed, pulling on my pants and buttoning my shirt.

Meanwhile, Jacob said something I couldn't hear.

I looked at him and he repeated himself.

"Vicki and I played that tape again. My idea. We were listening and then," he gestured, "she was *gone*. Vanished."

"You played it again? Why?"

"I wanted to know what happened before. We tried listening again, and Vicki disappeared. Poof! Gone!"

Jacob stared at a window sill for a moment.

"Waited all day for her to come back like you did, she has not reappeared yet. Still gone, but no puff of smoke. Quiet."

"How long?" I looked at my watch, looked again, it was 10 PM, Tuesday night. I'd slept for two days. Jacob stood up. "Don't go running off and do something stupid. Let me get some food, and we'll see about getting Vicki back. Alright?" He nodded. "Good. Where's the kitchen?"

The microwave warmed the water, the instant coffee dissolved quickly. Jacob sat, staring into the Minoan-shaped cup, Iroquois Casual China, while I hunted for cereal. Cornflakes was all he had. While I ate, he told me what they'd done: he and Vicki had sat up talking about what had happened when I listened to the music.

In the morning they returned to the basement, turned the instrument on, and replayed the tape with the lights on. A minute or so into the performance, Vicki vanished. For one second she was sitting in the chair, head back, eyes closed, the next the chair was vacant, and she was gone.

"Alright, you've said all that before. What did you decide about what had happened to me?"

"We did not. Vicki had some crazy notion she would not share with me, some nonsense about alternate worlds, Chinese ivory spheres, different planes of experience, plasticity of reality, I do not understand what she really was talking about.

Think she wanted to go where you went. Poof! She was not there any more . . . ."

"All we can do is try to follow. Repeat what happened to me as closely as possible." At the basement door. "Are you coming? She may need help to get back—we don't know what happened to her."

Eventually, I had to drag him downstairs.

"Turn the red dial until the VU meter is at around sixty cycles. Then turn all the switchboard dials to read at . . . nevermind. It will not work."

"How?"

Jacob stood and pushed me back from his machine. I sat in a chair, watching him manipulate the shiny chrome and black plastic instrument. Gold and silver connections glistened, wires, coded by thin lines of color flowed from one part to another. It was a beautiful machine composed of hard surfaces and black emptiness contrasting against the flow of wires and the sparkle of connections.

It was a complex animal made from many pieces, together more than any alone. And Jacob moved at the center—a spider in a web of his own devising, so complex that it trapped him like his prey . . . .

The vision startled me back to reality as the

speakers hummed to life, then quieted.

It was time to begin.

*

Sliding notes, disharmonious, but all part of a single whole, the many melodies rose like an ocean driven by many winds to pluck at my clothes. I leaned forward and the winds became stronger.

Seconds passed . . .

The winds started pulling insistently, the sky spinning wildly, but ignored, while the waves crashed demandingly on the rocks, a beacon and a warning. A gray cliff rose out of the mist, the waves crashing against half its height. Above, a stone wall ran along the precipice.

Grabbing Jacob, I stood, feeling the wind grab and lift us away into the night of song. Spiraling, we soared up the cliff face away from the crashing ocean, up toward the top most part, to drift along, over the ruination of the ancient wall. Gray stones and waving grass passed beneath us as we soared along like birds, skimming scant inches above the wall itself, until we came to the gate.

Made from sticks tied together with twine and guarded by two dancing crustaceans, the gate swung open as my feet landed on the cobbled stones of the path leading back through fields of grass toward a forest in the distance. The winds died to a thin breeze rippling into the distance.

I walked through, Jacob following. A dancing dog ran toward us, tail wagging, "Take my tail; you *are* expected!"

Jacob and I looked at each other, then did as the dog said. As soon as we'd both taken hold, the dog leaped into the air, legs stretched out like a mountain goat with coarse gray-brown hair and large curving horns. Springing faster and faster forwards. I shifted my grip to the right horn, Jacob taking the left—the dog was now a goat.

The mountain goat continued to spring forward; far in the distance, I could hear the dog singing some song, but I couldn't make out the words. I tightened my grip, as I watched the lands beneath me speed by, blurred beyond any recognition. Finally we landed, and the goat began to run, feet moving so rapidly that they became invisible, horns curling like bicycle handle bars, covered with coarse tape that cut into my hands, as the wheels spun and spun, moving ever faster and faster, their rhythm provided by a pair of pumping feet perched on faster spinning pedals.

The dog pedaled ever faster. I looked over at him as he sat on the seat, smiling maniacally at us both, while we were hanging onto the handle bars like a pair of insane streamers, billowing in the wind.

Squinting, I could see that we were headed for some strange building that rose out of the ground, shaped like a colossal mushroom. We slowed and stopped at the door, the dog riding away laughing when Jacob and I let go of his bicycle.

I turned back to the house.

We've arrived — but where are we? I thought, looking at the door in front of me. It was a perfectly normal door, except that it was mounted in the base of a mushroom. A brass bell hung next to it, intricately engraved with the a garden scene where various groups of people played billiards on the grass or danced. I pulled the cord and waited, looking at Jacob who stood beside me looking dumbly at his right shoe; "Poof! Gone!" he whispered to it.

Then the door opened. The dog, still smiling showing all his carnivorous teeth said, "Come on in! What took you so long? We've been waiting simply *hours!* It's so nice to have company, don't you agree? But of course you do, otherwise you wouldn't have come!" He stepped aside, gesturing for us to enter. We did; he continued, "So how are things where you come from? No, don't tell me,

I know: the same, as always, right? Things don't ever seem to change around here at all, you know that? That's what makes having visitors so nice, don't you agree? Of course you do . . ."

I stopped listening and walked after him, watching him brush a speck of lint from his fine black suit. The marching after the dog gave me the first chance to think since Jacob woke me. As we walked, I realized something, again a second time: *I should not have come.* And immediately felt a wave of guilt wash over me. Somehow I was responsible. If I hadn't come, then none of this would have happened—it was really my fault that Vicki had vanished, at least in part. I resolved to find Vicki before Jacob realized that *too.*

The dog led us through the maze-like passageways, talking as he walked. We followed him, turning corners, climbing stairs until we finally came to a door, which the dog opened and gestured with a flourish for us to enter.

A courtyard was on the other side—green grass, cypress trees, blue skies, a dinner party, complete with dance band. I went in, and had to go back out to drag Jacob along.

Looking around, I saw everyone was wearing fancy dinner clothes, all fine suits and expensive dresses in white and red. No black. I felt very out of place dressed in only a shirt and slacks, until I noticed that I, too, was wearing a suit.

I don't know how it happened.

No one noticed us as we walked through the crowd, looking at people who seemed familiar, but not quite. *Is Vicki here?* I wondered looking around. I thought I saw her in the distance.

Moving toward a woman wearing a long, white dress with red belt, it looked like Vicki was just behind her. I reached out to get her attention as I said, "Excuse me, could I get past you?"

She screamed. Then she screamed again.

I saw Vicki turn toward us; saw Jacob grab for her hand; I ran for the door, weaving through the mess of people. An army of faceless men wearing police uniforms ran toward us from behind the trees. The door wasn't far away, as the men were getting closer. I looked back at Jacob as I dragged him along. He didn't have Vicki. He was crying. Then they grabbed us and something hit my head, leaving me to go spinning away on a sea of blackness, the finale of the song swelling up at me. Vertigo swept my feet out from under me, up and down trading places, each sliding into the other. The last thing I heard was Jacob say was *Poof!* and then it was dark. And I could feel the ground was hard, dusty. I groped until my hand found a step in the black. So I sat, looking out, seeing nothing. Then I realized I was on the bottom step in Jacob's basement.

"You out there?" No one answered, and I just waited with the certain knowledge that he was gone too.

HIDE AND SEEK

I hoped no one would notice the stench of benzene that I was sure was curling out from the small bag at my feet as I stood at the receptionist's counter in the hotel. If I didn't have a cold, the fear would be gone; I did and it wasn't. The porter came over and tossed my bags onto his cart. "I'll carry this one." I said when he reached for the small one.

He said very good, sir and went off to wherever they go, saying something about meeting me at the room. I turned to the key in my hand, *Room 1472 Carlton Hotel.* Toronto. Heading for the elevators, I got my first good look at the lobby: high vaulted ceilings, deep sound-swallowing carpeting, arches and gilt edges. The height of gilded age splendor. I wondered who else had arrived early, as I stood tracing the brass vines that wrapped themselves around the elevator doors.

Recalling the details never happens in order. Things get mixed up, run together. Life is never like the stories in books, a linear progression of one thing after another. The solution, if it ever presents itself for the mystery, always comes too late or too soon. There was some detail you missed, or some part that just didn't add up. And then, sometimes, there is no answer because you're asking the wrong questions, caught up in the progression, the minutiae of details, missing the big picture because when you do finally stop and look, what you thought you say wasn't there at all.

*

All families have their skeletons. Their pariahs and prodigal sons. The older families, such as mine, just seem to have more than most. One of ours had recently crawled out.

I am by profession a photographer, my life seems to be in pictures, but nevertheless, as I sit here writing this, the words are more appropriate than any pictures that I could take. Writing it all down was Miranda's idea—Great Aunt Miranda. She must have been born old, since even though I have known her for almost all my life, she has never changed, never aged, really. Always at the yearly Christmas parties, laughing, drifting from one group of grandchildren to another, handing out candies, with faces on the wrapper.

She was the sort who'd walk up and say, "Guess what I've got for you?" and then proceed to pull the candies out of thin air, or your ear, or a pocket you're sure was empty. Always doing her little tricks. Playing little jokes. She was one of the fixtures of the Christmas party, always there to make the youngest laugh, to make everyone smile.

She dragged me aside by the arm that first night: "You simply must write all this down. Must. Now, don't go saying 'I don't know how' because you do. So do so. And I want to see it when you've finished." Then smiling, she flitted away. Not the usual request—I wouldn't have thought she would ever ask anything of anyone, but to demand it? Very strange.

*

The Wedding came first. Then after, *The Hotel*. The family had agreed to have the reception at the annual get-together. Always the Hotel Carlton, always in Toronto, always December. I was puzzled by this particular tradition, but that's what a tradition is.

Silver and crystal covered all the tables in the room. I stood off to one side, not wanting to get too involved in the reception. I've always found them to be so boring; but, not fun, . . . interesting to watch as Great Aunt Miranda had people laughing on one side of the room; on the other, people stood in small huddles talking in earnest about something probably not as important as they made it, while in the middle the Family of The Groom cowered, not at all sure they wanted to get to know us.

But then Miranda saw me off to one side, looking bored, so she just reached out and pulled me in, taking me around the room on the current of her personality, giving introductions while perched on my arm, catching me up on all the family:

"See him, over there? That's your Uncle George. Been gaining weight lately, don't you agree? I heard he's been losing money. Playing the horses. Carousing in general. Not a bad sort really, just needs guidance. Don't know who's with him. Some blond he picked up, no doubt."

—And I was a little boy again, the favorite of Great Aunt Miranda, being led around the room, as she pointed out all the family.

—"I don't know what's wrong with him these days. Not been the same. And he's talking to Bernard again, no doubt up to no good, if you ask me. Those two are always bringing trouble onto the family. Always."

—She turned and pulled me in another direction before dropping me by the table with the melting ice sculpture and warm caviar. At least the champagne was chilled. I had just picked up my glass when Suzanne hid my eyes. "Guess who?"

"Let me see," I said, knowing who it was. Suzanne and I had been playing this game for twenty years, but I still wasn't allowed to guess right. It was against the rules. "Hmmm. The Pope?"

"No, it's me Suzanne!" She laughed, kissing me on the cheek. "Been a long time. Where were you last year? I missed you, we all did. Not the same without you or Miranda. You two're the life of the party."

Miranda missed last year, too? Strange, I thought she never missed. "Oh, you know how it is—I get lost in my work, and have to untangle myself for this. Last year, I just couldn't. Did you say Miranda wasn't here either? I thought she *always* came."

"Not last year. Everyone thought it unusual—neither you nor Miranda. It was a dead year. Not much happened, except for Uncle Robert."

*

Uncle Robert. All I remember of him is a large laughing man who liked to give unusual gifts to everyone. I hadn't seen him since I was five or six, but I remember his presents: ornately painted shadow-puppets from Java one year, the next, German wind-up toys. One per child. We raced them down the hallways at the Family home, built ages ago, and standing several miles from Quebec City. That's where we would be going, after the wedding. Weddings always and forever at the Carlton in Toronto.

Last year, Uncle Robert came home for Christmas and died.

*

"It's terrible." I said.

Suzanne nodded, looking solemn for a moment, then brightening again. It was unlike her to stay sad, even for a moment. "We're getting a game of Hearts together later, and you're joining us, aren't you!"

I nodded, she continued. "Wonderful! That means we've got enough to use two decks!" And then we were off: across the room to the other cousins. "Look who I found! He was off lurking in the corner. And I thought, what's he doing there?

Jason should be over here with us. So I went and got him."

Most of them I recognized, now a little older, a little heavier: Mark, who always seemed to be trying to get me in trouble when we were little; Kevin, who seemed to be helping; Katherine, who if you called her "Kate" would kill you; Persephone, always smiling, like Suzanne; Josephine, dark, brooding Josephine. I loved them all, even the ones I didn't know all that well."

"It's been a while." They nodded agreement. "I really hate to be morbid, but you were all here last year? Let me in on Uncle Robert. What'd he look like? I only vaguely remember him."

Mark frowned at me, but said, "He died. There's nothing more to say really. Must have been a heart-attack, a stroke. Something like that. Fell dead during dinner. Made a real mess. During the soup, spilt the bowl across the table, stood up and then collapsed, knocked Aunt Margaret right out of her chair. Good thing she wasn't hurt."

Katherine picked up from there. "I was sitting next to her. She just lay there on the floor, wailing and crying. It was awful. Ruined Christmas completely. But you should have been there to see the look on Jacqueline's face. I looked at her, first, you know, to see what she was doing. And for a moment. Well, it was a long way to the head of the table, but I thought I saw her *smile*."

Jacqueline was the great grandmother of us all; she ran the family. "*Smile?* You're kidding. Don't tell lies, Kate." Kevin said, sipping from his glass. "We don't need another incident. Oh, you don't know, Jason? Well, never mind. It's not important."

It took a moment to sink in, but then I remembered—Kevin and Katherine were brother and sister. We kept talking quietly, the Bride and Groom snuck off to their suite and the reception continued, without them. No reason to break up a good party, after all, just because the Guests of Honor had left.

*

Hearts is a game we play only when we have enough people to use at least two decks, and sometimes three. The play always goes something like this: we deal out the cards, and then spend our time accusing each other of cheating, or counting cards, or palming cards, or what have you. The game is lucky if we finish one hand. It's a good night if we get through two.

That night, we got through three.

*

My bags still stood to the side, mostly unpacked. The room was just like all the others I had stayed in: high ceilinged with fancy moldings, long and thin, ending with large windows that offer a view of the city that isn't all that interesting. The large suitcase would stay packed until we went south, to the family home. Two days after the wedding had passed; that was when the Bride and her husband would fly to Maui for honeymoon. We were waiting to see them off. Thus, no need to unpack for only a few days stay.

Except for the small bag—it I did unpack, setting the plastic bottles of fixer, developer, stop and the plastic pans in a small group on the table. The other bottles stayed in their own shock-resistant case: benzene, carbolic acid, hydrochloric acid. The camera and its lenses were sealed in baggies, my socks wrapped around them as padding. I had packed the camera bag in the larger suitcase, as an added precaution. I still don't trust airlines, even after flying most of my life. What clothes I did need were in the suitor, hanging from the bathroom door. I was going to bed, certain that my cameras and chemicals had survived the journey when someone knocked softly on the door.

I opened it, surprised to see Katherine standing

in the hall, shifting from foot-to-foot nervously. "We have to talk."

*

When I was fourteen Uncle Douglas had me help him move boxes down in the cellar, him leading the way through the aisles of boxes on shelves, past the wine racks, through the bins of discarded toys and shelves of lost or forgotten books to where the oldest things were: the chests, the furniture, the ancient cabinets. All covered by dust and hidden by dark shadows in dim light. It was here that we stopped.

"There's a secret in this box here I'm going to show you, but you must promise never to tell anyone where it is. They all want to know, but I won't tell *them.* But someone should know. Someone else." He led me back into the piles of furniture, through a maze worthy of Theseus, to a dresser with a dim, streaked mirror, with spots that reflected back only darkness. Uncle Robert pulled at the bottom drawer.

"You've got that torch, like I asked you to bring?" —I nodded—"Good boy. Now, shine it down in here, and tell me what you see."

I did what he asked, standing on tip-toe to look down into the deep, high drawer. In the bottom was a long thin metal box, a lock specked with rust holding it closed. "What is it?"

"Ah, so you do see it, then. That's good. Remember it, remember where it is, and most important. Don't tell anyone. Not anyone that you know about this. Especially your Aunt Margaret. Tell her, you might as well tell everyone yourself. It would save a lot of time. Aunt Margaret tells everyone everything, so don't let her know any secrets."

He grunted, and strained to lift the box out of the drawer. The floor boards protested as he set it on the floor, then pulled a bunch of keys from his pocket and unlocked it. He showed me what was inside, then relocked it, put it back in the drawer, and we went back upstairs.

I have forgotten what was inside, if I ever really knew.

*

Katherine sat in a chair, talking about anything, but why she'd come to pound on my door at four in the morning. I watched her play with the thin belt, cross then uncross then recross her legs under her brilliant green dress as she talked. Finally, after almost half an hour of her skirting the issue, she got to the point.

"It's about, well, it's about Uncle Robert. And Jacqueline. I heard them fighting about something the afternoon before he died. Something was wrong. We all knew it last year. It was in the air, even before he arrived. We weren't expecting him. We all knew something was wrong, when both you and Miranda didn't show up. Your call, then her letter. They got everyone upset. No not upset, edgy.

"We were all waiting for something to happen. You know, like in a horror movie, where you know that something just awful's about to happen, but you cant do anything. Like that. Everyone was just creeping around, ask anyone else, they'll tell you I'm right. I knew something like this would happen. My cards,"—she held up a pack of large cards, wrapped in a red silk scarf with a green border, Tarot cards, I guessed—"they even said something was waiting to happen. Then Uncle Robert . . . died. It was awful." She started crying, tears running down her cheek, softly.

"He never did anything to anyone, why should he die? She killed him, I know it! If she didn't then she had someone do it."

"Who?" I reached over to comfort her, but she jerked back.

"Jacqueline. Who else? I *know* you didn't. You

weren't there last year, you couldn't have. Poor Uncle Robert, everyone conspiring against him, I'm sure of it. You're smart. Real smart. Better than us all. I'm sure you can prove she did. I trust you." Katherine stood up, wiping at her eyes with a Kleenex. "I'd better be going before Kevin notices I'm gone. I'm telling the truth. Jacqueline killed Uncle Robert. *I know it.* Kevin'll say I'm having another 'incident', but I'm telling the truth. *Believe me.*" She went to the door. "Good night, I knew you'd help."

The door closed, she was gone.

I sat back in my chair, listening to the distant sounds of the night streets, the quiet hum of the hotel, the soft yowling of the northerly zephyrs as they passed my window. I went to bed with many half-formed questions fluttering around me like moths.

*

Breakfast was more a duty than a meal. Jacqueline would rise early, just to be the first into to the private dining room the hotel set up for us: a long table leaded with fruit, hot and cold cereal, juices, ham, etc. She would choose a table towards the center of the room, and the rest of us would arrange ourselves at spots around that table.

We could come in at any time, up to eleven. I walked in at 10:45, and received a dark glance from her, followed by a gesture to join her. I poured myself some orange juice, and sat down. "Good morning Grandmother"—to say Great Grandmother was to incur her disfavor; she was vain about her age—"I'm sorry I missed seeing you last night at the reception."

"Good morning. Yes, I went to bed early. I had a long day getting Pauline ready for her wedding." She smiled, a smile that was not exactly kind. "What has Katherine been saying about me? I know she went to see you last night. My room is just down from yours, and I heard her knock. Nobody knocks the same as little Katherine. Did she say I killed Robert last year? It does not surprise me that she would. Do not take her comments seriously: she spent the summer a year ago in a sanitorium. She tried to kill herself. Imagine that. She is both paranoid and a habitual liar.

"Take she says with a grain of salt. Personally, I would recommend a long spoon when dealing with little Katherine's words; she means well enough, but. Oh well, you understand. You always were a smart boy."

I nodded, "You always know what's going on."

The smile became softer, grandmotherly. "What have you been doing with yourself? I haven't heard from you in ages. Tell me about Philadelphia."

I did, and the morning passed quickly and pleasantly, except for the brief lecture about Katherine and what she said. I remember a commercial that was on for a while, asking the question, 'Who Do You Trust?' I don't know. Not anymore. Paranoia is hard to shake once it grabs you by the throat.

*

Miranda came over, while the hotel staff clanked plates, and bumped metal trays together, laying out lunch. "Excuse me, Mother, but you can't keep Jason all to yourself. The rest of us haven't seen him for a year." Then, the lead me away to another table, I looked back at Jacqueline smiling to herself, as she leaned back into her chair.

Katherine smiled at me as she walked past, joining her father, Uncle Bernard and the Blond. George was already there. "Who's that blond?" I said, gesturing toward the table. Bernard saw and smiled back at me.

"His newest floozy. I think he said Ruth or Ruby or something last night. If you ask me, she's no good. Did you know her ears are pierced twice? Imagine." We sat, and I poured us glasses of ice water from the pitcher in the middle of the table.

I nodded, looking around the room. The water chilled my teeth. The Family came in, taking tables, waiting for lunch to be brought in: Mark and Kevin at one table; Persephone and Josephine sitting with their mother, Aunt Margaret and her husband, Uncle Douglas—all four looked like something was wrong. Then I noticed who was missing: "Where's Uncle Samuel? I haven't seen him."

"He's here, somewhere. But you know, I haven't seen him since the wedding. I heard he'd taken up with someone around here. Not at all sure it's a woman, either, if you know what I mean. He's lucky Mother hasn't heard, yet. But she will, mark my words, and when she does. . . . Anyway, at least Mark's come out alright, even if he does spend most of his time sitting around the house. Thinks he's a painter, but if you ask me, he'll not sell any of what he does. Just dabbles, really. He's been trying to get me to sponsor him at one of the galleries, my galleries, but I'll not have him there."

"Too bad. I would have thought he'd have inherited at least some talent."

"No, he didn't. When we get home, you ask to see some of his work, then you'll know. Not exactly bad, but not really any good either. Average, and maybe a little lower." Miranda looked down at the plate the waiter had just set before her. "Oh good! They *did* do the bluefish after all! You'll like this—I've been trying for ages to get Mother to let us all try it. It's the best."

A puddle of yellowish sauce with green specks smothered a slab of fish, garnished with small red onions. I hoped Miranda was right.

*

Katherine insisted I go with her after lunch to the museum of china and glass. It was a small building, built of brick and a welcome rescue against the wind that screamed through the streets outside.

Inside it was not exactly dark, just a bit dim, and warm. We wandered through the exhibits, looking at the china cups and saucers, the Rococo statues of lute and lyre players, the glass bowls. Katherine said very little beyond pointing out a detail here, a dancing child there. I wondered what had happened, she clearly wanted to say something; what I didn't know, but was going to find out.

On the third floor, standing in front of a case of bottles. It seemed as good a time as any to get to the point: "What's the problem?" A simple enough question, I thought.

Katherine looked at me, then said, "What did Jacqueline tell you about me? That I'm crazy, that I'm not to be trusted—a compulsive liar, unable to ever tell the truth?" —I nodded—"I thought so. Don't you see? This just proves my point, that she killed Uncle Robert! Why else would she, you know, need to tell you horrible things about me, unless she's hiding her murder?"

I shrugged. "I can think of another reason, but you don't want to hear it. She also said you're paranoid."

"Just because I don't want to play the stupid games she sets up. *She's the one who's crazy. Not me.* Come on, you'll like the chess set—it's one of my favorites."

She led the way, I followed.

*

I hate airports. I hate being in airports and I hate going to airports. Pauline and her husband were flying to Maui. I went to the airport, riding with Bernard and his blond in the BMW. I went because everyone else went, and I was expected to. "I'm sorry, but I never did get to meet you. I'm Jason."

Her hair was pulled back, into a ponytail, as if she was a ten-year-old. She looked about thirty. "Ruth," said Bernard, and she giggled. Looking at her I realized she wasn't really blond, but had bleached her hair.

Bernard continued. "I met Ruth here, down in Vegas. Isn't that right?" —another giggle—"She's my goodluck charm, I just rub her ass whenever I need a bit more. And I always get it. And if I don't well, there's other places to rub that work even better." He winked at me. I hate airports. Bernard wasn't helping in the least. "You know, son, get yourself a lucky charm, and everything's gonna go your way. Always does. Telling that to George last night. Lucky charms. Everybody should have one."

"I heard you two've got some business deal in the works. How's it coming along?"

"Yeah, me and George. But it's all hush-hush,

you know."

"Yes." The conversation ended there, silence except for the noise of the road, the car until we reached the airport. We parked in a group, then headed off to find the gate; the bags were sent ahead.

Laughter followed us as we walked along in a large group, Jacqueline's vanity lost out to her age, and she rode along in a wheelchair, Mark pushing, and not looking too happy about it. *He doesn't like her,* I thought, seeing the pair. *Why would that be?*

At the gate, just before boarding, Pauline jumped in front of me, saying mock-sternly, "Jason, kiss the bride goodbye!" I did, and as we hugged, she whispered in my ear: "Watch out." Then moved on to someone else.

*

Fortunately for me, the ride to the estate from the hotel was with Aunt Margaret and Uncle Douglas, Persephone and Josephine (their daughters). We took the limousine that Pauline and Jacob—I found out his name as he shook hands, then left—had ridden in to the dreaded airport.

"I hear you're a photographer." Douglas said, as he poured himself a second scotch on the rocks. "Some kind of artist, right, like Ansel Adams?"

"More like Bernice Abbot or Eugene Atget. Documentary, not landscape."

"Oh." He refilled his glass. "Never heard of them. They any good?"

"I've heard of them," Margaret tried to hide the dark look she gave Douglas, failed. I hoped they weren't going to argue the whole trip down; it was late and I was tired. Airports always do that to me. "They're both real good. Didn't Abbot work with Man Ray in Paris?"

"*Him* I've heard of. Not those other two. Mustn't be too good if I've not heard of them."

Perhaps Bernard wasn't such a bad idea, after all. "Well, they're kind of obscure. But that's because nobody cares too much about Documentary-type photographs. Those I do because I like to, but I also do others. When we get to the house,

Jacqueline insisted I show my portfolio. You'll get to see them then. I didn't want to, but she insisted."

"Jacqueline. Bitch. We should all yell 'Seig Heil!' when we see her. She acts the tyrant enough. A dictator if you ask me."

"Douglas! Nobody wants to hear what you have to say about my grandmother, so just be quiet."

He grunted but was quiet. I decided to change the subject. Maybe Uncle Douglas would pass out soon. I hoped so, I always avoided him when I was a child, because he smelled funny; it was just as well that I didn't get too close. He spent most of his time complaining about something or other to anyone who'd listen. The few times I did get near him, a long lecture about how awful whoever he didn't like at that time would follow. "I heard Uncle Robert came back last year."

Persephone looked up, startled. "Yes, he did. Said he wanted to play Santa again, and give us all his presents personally: he'd brought us all Viennese Chocolates. They were great—fresh and sweet. Chocolate covered fruit, even. They were the best!"

Josephine nodded, brushed a troublesome brown hair out of her eye, "I ate mine the first night. You should have been there. It just isn't the same without you or Aunt Miranda. Not in the least."

I smiled at that, I'd been hearing it often enough. "It's terrible what happened. Wasn't there any warning? I mean, people don't just *suddenly* die, that's just too terrible to think about." Curiosity got the better of me.

"I didn't like him, not at all. Even for an in-law he was a bad man. Awful man, really. Couple of days before, was were in that monster library, having a little drink, and in comes he said to me that his watch alarm went off, nasty little thing; hate those watches with all the little buttons and lights. Can't even tell time those things."

"He was on medication?"

"What? Oh yes. That's what I was saying. Heart pills."

*

Daniel fell. The estate is very old; how old, I don't know. I remember running through the gardens during the summer evenings when the first wisps of fog would drift between the tree trunks and across the fish pond. The marble statues would seem to move in that mist, taking on a life of their own, as in Atget's photographs. That was the time I liked—when the light just started to fade and the garden would seem alive with dancing people, satyrs, nymphs.

We would play our games in that mist, running around the trees, statues, trying to scare each other. Until the day Daniel, the youngest, climbed up the tree, and fell. I saw it happen. Everyone else was busy with other things. I watched him point at something in the distance, saying "Jason, you've got to see this, but keep it secret. Come on up. Look at that!" He pointed; his weight shifted; he fell.

By the time the Family arrived, it was all over. The cousins shifted back and forth on the edge of the garden, looking at the tree, the broken limbs. Katherine was crying. Miranda stood and watched a moment, then took us inside. On the way she handed Katherine a tissue, and pulled me aside. "Were you with Daniel?" —I nodded— "What happened? You can tell me, it's not your fault Jason. Nobody blames you."

"He fell. Daniel's dead, isn't he?" The tears began.

"Yes."

"I don't want him to be dead. I miss him."

"I know. How did he fall, you know, don't you?"

"Yes." And then I lied. Whatever Daniel saw, it was secret: "He slipped off the branch."

"Alright, better go with the others," Miranda said. After that I got special attention. From Miranda. Children, especially young children are resilient, amoral, monstrous.

*

Pauline had stuck a folded piece of paper into my coat pocket before she left. I got my first chance to look at in my room on the third floor. From the door, nothing seemed to have changed—the desk still had the piles of papers and books, the jacket I'd left lying on the back of the desk chair still lay where I'd left it. The blinds were still closed, and the faint chill of a room left empty for a long time hung in the air. I set my bags by the door. I wanted to know what Pauline's note said.

But I wasn't going to find out. Suzanne pushed the door open, and knocked on the frame.

"Knock-Knock. Anybody home? Come on, Jason. Katherine's got her deck out, and we're doing readings!"

"Just a moment." I picked my jacket up, noticing that it needed brushing. "Let me take care of this, and I'll be along in a minute, alright?"

"Of course! I'll wait for you right here." I picked up the clothes brush, took care of the jacket. I noticed there wasn't a crease from where I'd left it on the chair-back. I thought there would be. "Come on, they'll start without us. We don't want to miss it."

"Coming." The jacket was clean. I put the note in my pocket and we went downstairs, passing the other rooms, their doors open, suitcases left beside them by the staff. A maid was dusting a table, and as we went past I stopped. Suzanne gave me an anxious look, and I decided my question could wait.

*

Someone was always in the Game Room. Tonight, it was full—almost everyone was there: Jacqueline, Miranda, Margaret and George were at a table playing Parcheesi; Katherine and the other cousins were off in a dim corner doing Tarot readings, while Bernard and Ruth played chess. On my way past, I glanced at their game. Ruth was winning.

During the long summers, we played games. In the winter, the games were more complicated, but the Rules were simple, and always the same:

> 1. *Play the Game.*
> 2. *Win the Game.*
> 3. *Play the Game again.*

Nothing else seemed to matter, except winning. Not even the game, itself. We pulled up chairs and caught the tail end of Marks reading. Katherine was pointing at the last card, a single cup, turned upside down. "This is the final outcome, it's a good card, but here it's reversed. Meaning, instability, reversal. Probably a major change in the present state of things. Oh, don't look so sad—it's not all that bad. You remember last year—much, much worse." She smiled hopefully.

Mark shrugged, then smiled. "No need to take it too seriously, after all." I sat back in my chair, watching the goings on as Katherine did another reading, then another. It was my turn.

"Here, shuffle the cards, cut them three times to your right, then give them to me."

I did as she said, then handed the oversized deck of cards to her and she began laying out the reading. I didn't pay too much attention to how she did that. Then she began to say what it all meant: "The present's shown in the 5 of Swords, meaning that there's problems ahead, coupled with the Moon. Not a good sign: these problems are caused by hidden enemies, deceptions and unforeseen perils. But there is hope—the goal against these problems is favorable, the 7 wands, success and courage against these problems. The need for approval is in the far past, while more recently there is a loss of home. The reversed 9 Pentacles shows that clearly." Katherine was starting to look slightly worried. "In the future is the reversed 10 of cups. Another bad card. There's a loss of friendship and a chance of family quarrels ahead. Do you want me to continue? Things don't get much better."

"Up to you, I don't mind, either way."

"We'll stop." I looked across the layout at the last card, the final result: The High Priestess. I knew what that one meant—unseen outcome, unknown future. Another bad card, in a bad reading. I watched Katherine shuffle them into the deck, trying to lose them. The mantle clock softly chimed eleven thirty. Katherine jumped. "I don't want to do anymore readings tonight. I'm going to bed. Good night. Good night, everyone."

And she left, wrapping and rewrapping the cards.

I looked at everyone around the table. "Game of *Hearts?*" Most nodded, Persephone stood, said good night and went to bed. "It's been so long, um. Better show me where they're kept."

Mark laughed. "Easy enough—in the cabinet by the fireplace. Better bring two decks." He pointed across the room, behind me. Turning, I saw and went to get them. The game lasted about an hour before it broke up, and we all went off to bed.

*

The ceiling was lit by a strange crisscross pattern of thin lines. I lay under the covers, my toes cold, listening to the wind whisper around the house, and a tree tap against the wall. Faintly, I heard a clock chime once, twice, three times: three AM.

I gave up. I wasn't going to get any sleep.

Downstairs, the hall was dark, tiny safety

lights lit small spots, giving the furniture in the long room strange shadows, hiding everything under a dark blanket. I threaded my way through the obstacle course slowly, carefully. Most of the furniture had moved since I last walked through late at night. I tried to remember where the library was.

A soft blue Persian carpet absorbed my footfalls when I entered. The glass-fronted cabinets held faint reflections of moonlight. Looking in from the doorway, the room was very still, very quiet, only the clock ticking interrupting the silence. Somewhere a board creaked. I switched a lamp on, banishing the moonlight out the window. The voice startled me; I thought I was alone:

"What took you so long?" The voice came from a chair, and I recognized it: Mark. "Been waiting for almost three hours. Didn't you get my note?"

I looked confused. It was easy—I was.

"Gave it to Suzanne, and she said she'd give it to you when she went to get you. You didn't get it?" —I shook my head no—"Said she would. Maybe she forgot. Not likely. Too late now. Besides, you're here. Wait a minute. If you didn't get my note, then why are you here?"

"Couldn't sleep, came down to get something to read."

He nodded, turned on the light next to him. "Just as well that I stayed so long then. I need a favor." He sat back in the chair, and removed his glasses to clean them. "You and Miranda're close. Am I right? You can get her to give me a try, can't you? My work needs showing. And I need the money. Besides, Miranda has all those galleries. I know it's a lot to ask, but will you?"

I paused, looking at the aging glass in the bookcase doors. "I don't know if she'll listen to me. She never has in the past." I tightened my robe, suddenly the room felt very cold.

"Look, give it a try, please?"

I nodded, then I had an idea. "Tell you what. I'll see what I can do for you with Miranda, and you'll tell me about last year's party. Deal?" I felt like Monty Hall. Mark would jump at it; it seemed like something for nothing.

"Sure. Nothing to tell, but if you want to know, I'm happy to tell you." He looked through the lenses at the lamp, then put his glasses on again. "Well, where should I start? We'd all known for about a week that Miranda wasn't coming. Then you phoned. Katherine got uptight about something. Don't know what. Said something about 'bad vibes'. I don't know.

"Anyway, Robert arrived on Thursday, I think.

The tenth. And died three days later. Other than that, not much happened. Why do you want to know?"

"Curiosity, I guess. I've been gone just two years, and when I get back, not only has an uncle I've not seen in twenty years returned, but he's died. That makes for a lot of happenings to miss. Feels like I've been gone for a decade."

"Oh."

A minute passed.

"Uncle Douglas said something about heart pills. Do you know anything about that?"

Mark started to shake his head no, then he stopped, and took off his glasses. "Wait a moment." He rubbed then with his shirt, looked through them, then scratched at a dark spot with his fingernail.—I sensed he was playing for time. *What did he know?*—"Yes. There was something. The morning before he died, he asked me where Dr. Franklin was. Said he needed a refill. That's all."

I nodded. "Anything else?"

"No. Why?"

"It just seems like you're leaving something out. That's all."

"*I'm* not. Now, have you got anymore questions? Or can I go to bed?" Mark started to get up.

"Actually, just one more question. Was there a fight between Robert and Jacqueline in here, before he died?" I sat back in my chair, hoping the shadows would hide the smiles I was sure were in my eyes.

"Fight? What fight? I wasn't . . . who said there was?" Honest confusion-surprise, or good acting, I couldn't tell. I opted for the former. Good acting it was.

"I don't remember. Someone mentioned it in passing. Maybe Margaret or Miranda. I don't remember. Either way, it's not that important."

"Good night. You will talk to Miranda for me?" Mark stood, and slouching, headed towards the door.

"Yes, I'll try." I decided that I would.

"Thanks." The door closed.

*

I went downstairs, passing through the game room to the hallway. I could hear Douglas snoring in the Library as I went past. Otherwise—the clock chiming 2, echoing down the polished hall—I was alone in the quiet.

Several hours had passed, and everyone had disappeared: the remains of lunch still sat out in the dining room, dirtied plates still to be cleared away.

A woman grabbed me from behind, holding her hands over my mouth and eyes. "Guess who?"

"Beelzebub?"

Laughter: try again.

"If it's not Beelzebub, then it must be someone worse. Now who do I know that's worse?" —I paused—"Suzanne?"

She laughed, letting me turn around. "Right! We're all getting ready to play a game. Want to join us?"

"What's the game?"

"Hide and seek! I even got Auntie Em to play along! It'll be wonderful! I was just coming to get you. . ."

"Ok. When do we start?"

"We already have. You're it!" And she ran away, her soft shoes making only the occasional squeak on tile.

I was alone again. And I was "it."

*

Ten years after the summer Daniel died, I remember waking up in the middle of the night to hear Uncle Douglas singing loudly, drunkenly, in the courtyard below my window. I lay in bed, too half-asleep to get up and go look. I don't think he was alone. He sang an old English drinking song loudly:

As I came home on a Monday night as drunk as drunk could be,
I saw a horse outside the door where my old horse should be,
Well, I called me wife and I said to her, will you kindly tell to me,
Who owns that horse outside the door where my old horse should be?
Aah you're drunk you're drunk, you silly old fool, for sure you cannot see,
That's a lovely sow that me mother sent to me.
Well, It's many a day I've traveled a hundred miles or more,
But a saddle on a sow sure I never saw before.

And as I came home on a Tuesday night as drunk as drunk could be,
I saw a coat behind the door where my old coat should be,
Well, I called me wife and I said to her, will you kindly tell to me,
Who owns that coat behind the door where my old coat should be?
Aah you're drunk, you're drunk you silly old fool, for sure you cannot see,

That's a woolen blanket that me mother sent to me.
Well, it's many a day I've traveled a hundred miles
*   or more,*
But buttons on a blanket sure I never saw before.

And as I came home on a Wednesday night as drunk
*   as drunk could be,*
I saw a pipe down by the chair where my old pipe
*   should be,*
Well, I called me wife and I said to her, will you kindly
*   tell to me,*
Who owns that pipe down by the chair where my old
*   pipe should be?*
Aah you're drunk you're drunk, you silly old fool, for
*   sure you cannot see,*
That's a lovely tin whistle that me mother sent to me.
Well, it's many a day I've traveled a hundred miles
*   or more,*
But tobacco in a tin whistle sure I never saw before.

And as I came home on a Thursday night as drunk as
*   drunk could be,*
I saw two boots beneath the bed where my old boots
*   should be,*
Well, I called me wife and I said to her, will you kindly
*   tell to me,*
Who owns them boots beneath the bed where my old
*   boots should be?*
Aah you're drunk, you're drunk you silly old fool, for
*   sure you cannot see,*
They're two lovely geranium plants that me mother
*   sent to me.*
Well, it's many a day I've traveled a hundred miles
*   or more,*

But laces in geranium plants sure I never saw before.

*And as I came home on a Friday night as drunk as
        drunk could be,*
*I saw a head upon the bed where my old head should
        be,*
*Well, I called me wife and I said to her, will you kindly
        tell to me,*
*Who owns that head upon the bed where my old head
        should be?*
*Aah you're drunk, you're drunk you silly old fool, for
        still you cannot see,*
That's a fine new baby boy that me mother sent to me.
*Well, it's many a day I've traveled a hundred miles
        or more,*
*But a baby boy with his whiskers on I never saw be-
        fore.*

At the time I thought it was funny; now, I'm
not so sure. Douglas wasn't alone. That song was
sung for somebody, I just don't know who is was.

*

When I was little, Uncle Robert was my favorite Uncle, always giving the best, most fun gifts. That was my childhoods criteria for judging the Family; most of them I only saw at Christmas, since most of the year was spent at American boarding schools, then American universities. Judging people by how good their gifts are is not a very good way to judge character, I know, but that is how children judge adults: do children see people differently than adults, or merely see different people? As we move forward through life we gain pains—hurts—caused us by the people we meet. In many ways, these pains are like cuts: some are small, thin; they hurt a lot, but pass quickly. Others reach deep, and cause slow torment over years; these wounds fester, and bite deep until finally the wounded collapses and dies. This is called growing up, and it lasts forever. The day Uncle Robert left he gave a second gift to all of us cousins. I was still six; it was scarcely three months after Daniel fell to his death, and two before my birthday. It was afternoon, and the light was starting to fail: changing the reds and yellows of autumn to a bloody red. We all stood in the foyer. Robert came in, shutting the door on a gentle breeze that carried a few dead leaves with it. And he handed out small boxes, wrapped in gold-colored foil, tied with white ribbon. "I want you to open these tonight. After dinner. Alright?" We nodded; he left.

It was the last time I saw him alive.

*

The cellar always scared me when I was a child. I hated to go down there alone. Always dark, always dusty, always dry. Walking alone down there, the blood gushing in my ears, footsteps echoing, strangely muted. Odd shadows. Odder things casting the shadows. And a wolf at the foot of the stairs, to scare away all intruders: a Cerberus to keep the kiddies out.

I seldom got farther than that stuffed wolf, perpetually snarling at the stairs, the first thing you see when you go down there. And if that wasn't bad enough, the cellar was a world of its own. Large areas of smooth concrete, empty except for a lone lawn chair, a relic of 1920. Rows of metal shelving, filled with boxes, books, things. All of them labeled carefully.

And beyond all these shelves, oases of space, racks with old clothes hung carefully in plastic cases, moth balls filling the bottoms, shelves of boxes, was the furniture. Heaps of furniture arranged with no mind to any order. In that mess there were even more secret spots, hidden treasures, lost desires, forgotten things. And a box that Uncle Robert showed me, once, long ago.

With an order to remember that I haven't followed.

*

It was in the hallway to my room that the thought struck me: right between the low glass case of Father's pistols, and the old flag. I wasn't sure, but something about Margaret's screaming struck me as wrong. Margaret wasn't the screaming type, not over anything. Not even her brother falling on her and dying. Not Margaret.

I turned back, looking along the long line of closed doors. *Which one was Marks?* But then I decided not to ask him; to ask Katherine instead. She would tell me the truth—I wasn't sure I trusted Mark for that.

Third on the left, past the potted geranium by the window.

The geranium was gone, but the window hadn't been moved. I counted three down, then knocked on a door I hoped was right; it was.

Katherine looked at me. "What? It's almost four in the morning." That she should complain about that struck me as comic for a moment. I smiled.

"Sorry. I really need to know something, and I need to know it now. The night Uncle Robert died, you were sitting next to Margaret, or Robert?"

"Robert."

"Ok. Run through what happened, again."

"Now? Can't this wait for morning? I'm still asleep." She turned back toward the bed, starting to close the door on me. "Talk to me later. Can't you do that?"

"It'll only take a moment." I stepped into the room and closed the door. "I don't want anyone to hear. Jacqueline sleeps lightly, she said so herself, but I don't know about the rest of them. Luckily, she's not on this floor. It's important. I'll be gone before you know it."

"You're right. Ask away."

"Robert. Did he say anything? Anything at all?"

"No. Now go to . . . wait. Yes, I think he did. Mumbled something as he fell. I don't know what, maybe Margaret does. Go ask her. I want to go to sleep; GET OUT."

I got.

*

Morning broke, and so did the cold. The thermometer soared into the fifties, and the thin snow that covered the grounds began melting, changing them into a mixture of dead grasses, old leaves and mud as I crossed the courtyard to the small cottage that huddled on the fringes of the main house. Once one of several grounds keepers' homes, now it housed Doctor Franklin. Or so I thought when I pounded on his door at ten am.

I didn't recognize the man who opened the door, but he knew me. "*Guten morgen*, Herr De Vantongerlou. You are Jason, *ja*?" He spoke with a heavy accent. In the background I could hear *Au Tannenbaum* playing. The man was in his late sixties or early seventies.

I said the only think I could think of, "Um."

Followed by something I hoped wouldn't make me seem any dumber than I already did: "I'm sorry, but I don't know who you are. Who are you?"

"Ach, I am the doctor. Doctor Ogden."—He held out his hand, soft, slightly damp.—"Your grandmother hired me this spring past to take care of happenings."

"You mean Jacqueline?"

"Yes. But do come in, not right for me to have

you standing out in the cold wetness. What have you come so late in the morning about? Not sick I should hope." He smiled, helpfully. I wondered about his fluency.

"No. Were you here when Robert died, last year?"

"Nein—no. I was not. It is terrible, *ja*, that one should die at such a moment. I have words with your Grandmother, she tell me what happens. The Herr-doctor Franklin, he leave after Robert dies, told 'go' by her. She blame him for it." His accent was quite ridiculous. There was no way he was really German. It was an accent for a villain in a B-movie.

"Oh." I paused, indecisive about the door and leaving. "Could I see his records? His medical records—perhaps you could explain what was wrong with him."

"*Ja!* I mean, yes. It is good to have company here. Very little for me, your family has health." Gesturing for me to follow, he led me through the first floor, toward the filing cabinets where the records were kept: through a sterile white hall. On the way he closed an open door, where *Tannenbaum* was playing, but not fast enough to hide the small portrait of Hitler. "Here we are. The records room."

"Where in Germany are you from?"

"Nein. Ich bin nicht . . . Sorry. No. I am not from Germany. From Austerich. Austria." He opened a drawer and pulled out a thin file. "This what you want." He handed it to me.

"What you see? You not tell anyone about me?"

"About what? I don't care if you're a Nazi or not. Just don't go bothering anyone about it."

"I was not part of the Jew removal. I was a little boy."

"Whatever." I wanted out. "Can I take this with me?"

He nodded; I did. Perhaps he wasn't playing *Au Tannenbaum*, after all. The *Red Flag* was the same music, but very different words.

*

The file was too thin. I knew that the moment I saw it. Which raised the question: who took what was inside, and why? The number of questions just kept growing the more I looked. Somehow, that seemed a bad sign. I read the file anyway, sure it wouldn't tell me much. Only that Robert was born, lived 53 years and then died. Of *Natural Causes*, whatever they were.

It was time to take a walk and have a talk with Aunt Margaret about Uncle Robert and the night he died. I found her in the library, the morning sun chasing away all the shadows of the night before. I got the feeling they were only hiding, though, waiting for their chance. "Aunt Margaret? Are you busy?"

"No, not really." She sat her book on the table, and looked at me expectantly. Waiting.

I sat down. "Could you tell me about Uncle Robert? I missed everything last year, and I never really knew who he was. He left when I was still only about six."

I would never have seen it, if it weren't for the bright sun light: she paled, for an instant, then recovered. "There's not too much to tell. He was my brother, even if we were never that close. He was twelve years older than I was, after all. With that much difference in ages, you can never be all that close." She paused. "What did you want to know?"

"The night he . . . died . . . what did he say to you? I heard that he mumbled something as he fell, and it wasn't *'Rosebud.'* I hate to be so abrupt, but what was it?"

"I really can't say. As you said, he mumbled. I didn't understand a word he said that entire evening. Just sat there real quiet, as if there was some problem he couldn't say. I would ask him things . . . how he liked being home. And he'd just mumble an answer. I don't know. Sorry." She smiled at me. Somehow familiar, that smile. I wondered where I'd seen it before.

"What about earlier on. After he got back, you must have said something." *This is getting me nowhere.* Either Margaret knew something and wouldn't talk, or . . . . "Did you have a fight?"

"What? No. Definitely not." —I knew she was lying, the answer was too fast—"We never really fought about anything. Why would you think we had a fight?"

"I heard mention of a fight . . ."

"Well, it wasn't *me*. I had very little to do with Bobby once he got back." She picked up her book. "I hope you don't mind, but I just remembered promising to play Rummy with Pauline. You will excuse me?" And left me alone in the library, again.

Things kept going around in a circle. I was getting nowhere. But I was sure of one thing, if Robert wasn't killed, he sure was helped along the way. Everyone was hiding something. Margaret most especially. The question was, what?

As I sat being confused, a maid wondered in, quietly dusting the tables, and rubbing them to a high polish. She was doing the hallway outside me room the night before. "You. Ah, I don't know your name, sorry. But do you know if anyone's been in my room, third floor, near the . . ."

"Joan, sir. I'm sorry to interrupt, sir, but I know which room you mean. If you're asking if I've been in there, then the answer's no, sir. I don't know if anyone else has, though. I'm sorry about that, sir."

"Thank you, Joan. And you don't have to say 'sir' in every sentence to me. Alright?"

"Yes, sir."

*

My thoughts were on history as I sat in my chair—tall, cold, soft—midway along the right side. I felt Jacqueline's eyes on me. In my life the events of the present seem to grow out of events long past, some are flowers, beautiful—but momentary. Others bear that proverbial fruit. And still others are weeds, living for years, hard and possibly dangerous to uproot, when you can find them. Long before I became a photographer, I took hobby pictures, snaps of family, etc. They never were very good, but I did try to save them, though now I have no idea why I would want to. I was going after them when the lunch bell rang. The discovery waiting me would keep.

This was where all important decisions, if they weren't made here, at least were announced. The dining room manages to seem formal even when it isn't. Two ancient chandeliers hang over the table, cut curved crystal prisms and dew drops, brass fittings, golden fixtures. The table was slightly on the over-long side, white linen tablecloth hiding the swirls of the wood. This was where Robert died. Strange how a room can have so much history, that a death, any death seems trivial by comparison. Not even a marker left.

"When do we get to see these pictures you've been in Philadelphia for?" It was a quiet reminder that my promise wasn't forgotten; that I would be showing them, sooner than later.

Think. Better be a good reason. "Oh, I was just waiting for a good time. Perhaps after lunch?"

Jacqueline smiled, happily. She took a sip of the too cold—I knew—water. "A wonderful idea. I've been looking forward to these pictures of yours."

I nodded, and she passed onto other matters that I didn't really pay too much attention to. Instead, I thought about what I knew, knew for certain about last year, and the death. The list was short, far too short for the amount of work I'd done:

(1) *Robert died during dinner.*
(2) *His medical records are gone.*

That's all of it. Two facts, many questions, and even the questions have questions . . . I was getting nowhere, an inept version of Sam Spade who couldn't intimidate a scarred field mouse into confessing.

Most of lunch had passed, when something caught my ear. Ruth was speaking, and it was the first time I'd heard her voice.

"Anyway, I was out for a walk this morning, it was so beautiful, the snow and the trees. Well, anyway, while I was out, I saw a really large building, all covered with snow, but still just oozing gloom and despair, like, Gothic. So I went over and, I've always liked ghost stories, and it seemed the place for one to lurk, hiding in shadows. Anyway, while I was there, I just thought, Ruth, take a look *inside*. So I did.

"You'll never guess what I saw!"

Mark said, "You were at the mausoleum. You saw tombs. I'm right, aren't I?"

"Nope! I looked in and I saw that someone else had been there too. Isn't that just horrible? They'd been there, and pulled one of those things on the walls, the plaque, off and left the coffin lying out in the middle of the room. It was disgusting! Smelled just awful. Anyway, I took just one look, and ran back here, and it was time for lunch, so I thought, I'd tell you afterwards. *That's* what happened to me this morning."

"How did you know that anyone had been there before you this morning?" I said. It was strange—seldom that anyone would go out to the mausoleum, even worse that it should be brought up. Jacqueline never approved of its mention. I glanced at her: she was interested, leaning back in her chair, pretending otherwise, but her eyes betrayed her; she wanted to know who was there as much as I did.

"The fool left his footprints, all over the snow." Ruth smiled triumphantly, and took a drink. "He must have forgotten about them, he was so busy digging someone up. The place was a real mess, you know? Mortar, plaster, cement, all that everywhere, and the coffin dragged into the center of the room, well back from the door—didn't see it until I got close. And it was still cold enough that there wasn't too much stink 'till I got inside."

"Jason, I think it would be best if we postponed your pictures until later. But I would like to talk to you. Excuse us." Jacqueline stood, and left, a little unsteadily. I followed after, saying excuse me. Something had happened, and I was going to find out what.

*

The garden was full of coffins. Stood on end, tall thin pine boxes surrounded by melting snow; they held the statues. It was strange to see the boxes, damp dirty things, standing in front of the hedges, or out in the grass where, during the summer months of my childhood, I would play in and among them: satyrs and nymphs looming out of the fog. They were gone, hidden, the grasses dead.

I hurried through, thinking back to what Jacqueline had said in her study, standing by the oak table with the bronze Mercury carrying his staff. While she spoke I had watched that statue, the twin snakes curling around the short stick, to face each other at the top. It seemed to be moving forward, bringing me some urgent message. "I would go myself, but I'm getting too old to go hiking across the estate in the dead of winter. But you can."

"And what am I supposed to find?"

Jacqueline turned from the window, and smiled—a thin, hard line. "Who was dug up. And by whom. Why." Picking up the statue, the smile vanished. "And when you know for certain, you are to tell me. Just me." The statue clicked against the surface of the table, a dismissal. *GO.*

I looked up from my thoughts at the mausoleum: oval, with a dome in the center. I stood at the door, wondering if it was locked. The vine leaves stood out clearly, marked by the white snow against dark bronze. The door scraped against the floor, sending a shower of birds into the sky, and I was inside.

The place stank (I could tell, even through my cold). And it was as Ruth said—littered with broken plaster, dust, cement. Ten or fifteen feet from the open crypt lay the coffin. The top was open; Robert's coffin was empty.

*

I saw what there was to see: 3 sets of footprints, all the same. Fairly average and made by notched hunting-boots, size ten; I sketched the notch patterns on a scrap of paper, then photographed them. They crossed from the door to the crypt, wandered back and forth through the rubble. Then moved to where the coffin lay—they must have carried it because one set left scuff marks, as if dragging his feet.

Ruth's footprints were entirely different, crossing the snow only slightly, a smudge here, there. She was trying to hide her presence inside, since it would have been easier to cross straight, but instead, her path must have wandered back and forth between the areas with snow. *Why?*

The answer would never be entirely clear and a long while coming.

I looked up through the oculus at the fading light: dark clouds gathered in the sky. Like dandruff, the first flakes of snow began to fall; I hurried back toward the house, hoping to arrived before it was fully night.

*

Thin moonlight lit the night air as I stood looking out the window next to my rooms door. Already, the courtyard below had a thin layer of snow, with more continuing to fall. A figure in a white coat ran from the house to Dr. Ogden's cottage, leaving long dark footprints in the snow. Then it was still again, the black tracks turning white.

I waited for the figure to return, to be sure of who it was. But it didn't. Not while I watched.

When the clock struck one, I ran down to check the boots in the coat room. Hangers made of wood held coats; boots stood on a low drying rack against the wall. Warm air hissed in the background, through a grill with a sailboat on it as I stood in the doorway. Wet footprints led from the outside door, in.

Pulling out my sketch of the footprints, I

crossed to the rack. There were eight pairs of hunting boots. Two size seven; six size ten. Of these, four were notched. I checked twice. None of them matched.

There was no white coat hanging up, either.

And none of the boots were damp.

*

Quiet echoed through the house as I stood in the hall, beside the chess set. Somewhere, distantly, a clock ticked. And the sound came again—Was it a footstep?—a board creaked softly. Light from up the staircase in the south wall filled the room with a dim glow. Harsh shadows. Quiet.

A third time, the sound came.

The light vanished; someone was at the top of the stairs. Standing, waiting, listening and maybe watching. I stood still.

Quiet, quiet, quiet.

A step creaked. The light flashed. Vanished again. Now a shadow was visible: dark legs, body on the floor. I wished I was near a light. Someone was coming downstairs.

"Look, I know you're there, so stop trying to hide it. Come down." I stepped to the stairs. "I'm tired, and don't want to play games."

The shadow remained still. Looking up, into

the light, I couldn't tell who it was. "Well?"

I blinked starting up, and the shadow vanished and the silhouette, too. Whoever was on the stairs wasn't there anymore. Or I was seeing things.

So I kept going. The hall was empty—long hard wood floor, closed doors, dimly lit stained glass window at the far end casting strange patterns of bright and dark toward me. It was cold, and I shivered.

The South Wing. I stood there, at the gateway to the forbidden area. Nothing but store rooms and private closets where the older family kept their secrets locked away. The doors were evenly spaced, six to a wall, opposite each other. It was dark, the only light coming from the stained glass window at the end. I stood, just watching, counting the seconds. Then the light came back, flooding the hall.

The clear parts of the glass were wavy; I couldn't see who was outside. The doors were locked, as expected. *What does this window look on?* I thought, pressing my forehead against the cold glass. Who was outside at one a.m., shining a spotlight on the South Wing? Why?

*

Margaret sat at the desk, turning the photo album pages slowly, sighing softly when I pushed my door open; I knew someone was there. "Yes? . . . Oh, Margaret, I wasn't. Um. Didn't know anyone was still up. Uh. . . . "I said intelligently, standing in my own doorway, an intruder.

"I wanted to speak to you. Who dug up Robert?" She stood, dropping the thick book with a thump onto the floor. "Jacqueline sent you to find out what happened, I want to know. First."

"Know? I don't know anything. Bunch of people pulled the coffin out, and left it on the ground. You heard what Ruth said. She covered about everything." I pulled the door closed after me. The spot made me paranoid—no need to help snoopers. "I really can't add anything. Sorry."

"Don't lie. We all know you're smarter than Bernard's current bimbo. So let's have it: what do you know?"

Shaking my head, I picked up the album, pushed it back into the shelf. "What do you know? Tell me, and I'll see if you've missed anything I know. Deal?"

"You first."

I ran my finger along the spines, counting: one—two—three—four—five—six—seven. All there. "No." I turned around; she stood looking at me through a mirror. "You heard what the deal was. Um. If you don't like it, well . . . um. You don't have to agree."

She nodded; I sat. Somehow I knew it was going to take a while.

And we sat. A minute passed. Margaret began rubbing at a spot on her hand. "What do you want to know? Where to start."

"Last year. Uncle Robert."

"Well, he came back. Gave out his gifts, then died."

"Look. I'm getting tired of everyone telling me the same brief bit. Now, give me all of it. Or else the deals off." I hoped she wouldn't call my bluff; I sat, watching her rub at her left hand.

She nodded to herself. "Alright. But you can't tell who told. Agreed?" —I nodded—"Bobby wasn't the most popular of us. Sammy never liked him; they were always fighting about something. When he came back, it wasn't any better than before. I don't know why he came back. I don't. I guess he felt guilty about Daniel. Who knows? Bobby always did keep things to himself. And his games. Those were what Sammy hated: Bobby's games."

"Games?"

"Oh. That's right—you didn't know Bobby that

well. Well, he liked games, the harder the better. Complex, ornate ones where the rules changed as you played. What'd he call his favorite? Oh yes, Idrazel, or something like that. No. That's not right. *Yggdrasil.* That was it. Never would explain what it meant."

"What happened last year?"

"He came back. It was just like he never left. I don't know what it was about, but they had a bad fight, and Jacqueline had to break it up. I'm not sure . . . ." She sat rubbing her hand. "I think I've sprained my wrist."

"Better get some ice. Come on, we can talk in the kitchen." I stood and we headed down.

The florescent lights flickered several times, then came on with an audible buzz. Our footsteps echoed down the room, a long thin place with a metal counter down one wall, stove at the end and white cabinets opposite. Ice wrapped in a towel, Margaret sat on a chair. "You're sure you want me to continue?"

"Yes."

She adjusted the ice, the plastic bag crumpling. Our voices echoed back softly. "Jacqueline didn't want to have to deal with the silly arguments between Sam and Bobby. She thought they were acting like children who hadn't grown up."

"You think Samuel killed Robert."

She looked up from her hand. *Yes.*

Margaret turned back to her hand. "I'm not sure. It must have been when I was lifting down some old boxes of books, earlier tonight. That's when it started hurting."

"Why not go see Doctor Ogden?"

"The NAZI? No, it'll be fine. I'll go into town and get myself a wrist brace later this morning. There are a few other errands to do also."

I nodded. "I think I might have an elastic bandage with me. Do you want it?"

"I'll be fine." She dropped the wet towel in the sink. "It's late, I'm going to bed. Good night." She turned and left.

"Good night." I looked out the window to see the thin snow still falling past darkness. Whoever went to see Ogden would be well hidden by morning, if not already. I went after the camera, sticking new batteries into the flash as I hurried for the door.

Perhaps not completely hidden.

*

Suzanne stood next to the light. It was very bright. "Mwrphl?" I grunted, looking up at her. She smiled.

"Good morning, get up or else you'll miss the trip! Aunt Margaret's going into town, and if you don't hurry, you'll miss it! Get up!"

"But I don't want to go . . . ."

"Yes, you do. Now come on." She went to the door, pulling it closed after. She left the light on. I would have to get out of bed to reach the switch. I would have to get up.

I pulled the covers over my head and tried to go back to sleep. A minute later Suzanne was back, still smiling. It took a moment before I noticed the glass of water she was holding. "Now, get up."

"Fine. I'm up." I sat up, chased her out, and considered going back to bed. It was a pity that all the locks had the same key. "I'll be along in a minute."

Suzanne was waiting outside the door. She still had her glass of water, but was drinking it. "You weren't really going to?"

She nodded. "Of course I would. Why not?" We went downstairs. "Everyone's waiting. Almost everyone. It's going to be fun."

"Fun. Is Uncle Samuel going to be coming down this year? I haven't seen him since the wedding."

"Hmmm? Oh yes. He's coming down. Going to arrive tonight—that's what he said. We'd better hurry."

I pulled my coat off the hanger, still damp from the night before. A white coat hung several hangers down. "Whose is that one," I said, pointing.

"Don't know." Suzanne dragged me across the yard. The four of us were on our way, and my hands were cold, even in my pockets. The crumpled piece of paper reminded me: I still hadn't read Pauline's note. And it would have to wait even longer. I decided to remember to look at it.

Persephone shivered. "Turn the heat up, Mom. It's still cold back here."

"Wait for the car to warm up. It won't take too long." Margaret said. Then, looking back over her shoulder, "Glad you could join us, Jason."

I nodded. "Didn't get much choice in the matter. Besides, I need to pick up a new enlarger lens. The one I had with me cracked on the ride down. Must have had a suitcase dropped on it or something."

"You brought the lens with you—I don't remember them knowing too much about cameras at that shop."

"Um, yes," I said, feeling the lump in my jacket. "It's here."

"There is a camera shop in town, isn't there? I think so."

Pauline nodded from the front seat. "On second, next to Martin's Hardware."

"We'll stop by before we leave."

"Thanks."

I watched the snow covered woods pass by, the occasional house until we reached the town. It wasn't as far as I thought. The camera shop was called "Jenkin's Camera" and was small. Shelves of arty frames to the left of the door, overpriced camera bags to the right and a glass counter in front. A clerk looked around a partition to say she'd be with us in a moment.

"How can I help you?"

I set the lens on the counter. "I need to replace this."

"Dropped you camera? That's a shame, but I think we've got something like this, eh? Just a bit. I'll go check." She went back into the rear. "You're in luck! Our last one." She set the box on the counter. "Gimme a moment to charge this up. You're from the states. I can tell. Where?"

"For the moment, Philadelphia."

"I've got a friend there. Maybe you know her?

Denise."

"No. I don't. Philadelphia's a big city."

"Too bad."

I handed her a credit card. Signed. Took my receipt and went back to the car where Margaret, Suzanne and Persephone waited. We went home. Something bothered me about the camera shop all the way back.

The lens. It wasn't a common type, but the store had one in stock—I'd had to order the broken one special while in Philadelphia. Why should a place out in the middle of nowhere, Canada have it? Paranoia is contagious—Miranda has shared her worries with me, and I could feel them coloring everything. Schizophrenia is a cognitive disease that develops from pathological thought process turning everyday ambiguity and coincidence into patterns that aren't really there. In schizophrenia, ambiguity polarizes into ambivalence, blocking the right, 'normal' solutions. I was getting a bit crazy. Or maybe I was right. Family does that to you.

*

We arrived back just after lunch, and Pauline's note sent me down to the cellar. A snarling white sheet stood guard at the foot of the stairs. The dim light was barely showed her map, across the top: "U. Robert left a box for you with me. When he died, I hid it in the cellar. *Don't trust anybody — U. Robert didn't die naturally. He was killed.*" in her flowing script. I grabbed a flashlight from beside the door and headed into the darkness.

Metal shelves filled with dark boxes, dusty furniture all passed by. The marks left by Pauline guiding the way, each one different, unique—the path was clearly marked only for me. Without her map, I would have been lost.

Kneeling, I turned the flashlight off, sticking Pauline's note deep into my pocket. Perhaps twenty feet away I could see my shadow's light. I worked my way closer, trying to see who: dark clothes, soft dark shoes. I came closer: a woman. Small feet, small hands: But who?

I was right behind her when she switched off her light, spun around and hit me with it. The floor jumped up and hit me, too.

She jumped over me, feet softly slapping the cement floor. By the time I was standing with my light, she was gone. I was alone with the dark silence; so I continued. The path led me into the deeper recesses of the cellar until I came to a box.

It sat on a metal shelf with other boxes, older water stained and age-spotted. Yellow. I couldn't have missed it. The light ran across the top, chasing a white spider. Smooth dust. I sneezed pulling it down.

The lid hit the floor with a thud. The box was empty.

Or so I thought; the inside was, but a letter in a white envelope "JASON" written across it lay on the box beneath. Sneezing again, I decided to read it someplace less dusty.

I stuffed it into my pocket, only to have it crumpling loudly as I ran upstairs to the land of the living. I turned to head back. As I passed the third mark, the lights went out. The guiding light of the ceiling lamps was gone. It was truly dark.

Then, from somewhere behind me—a footstep.

*

Fall came early when I was sixteen. It was middle August when the first thin snow fell, changing the green leaves on the trees yellow, orange, brown. Until that snow it was hot, the Estate shut down during the afternoon, everyone hiding inside, in the shade: Miranda on the porch, sketching with a stick of charcoal, or playing hearts, everyone too hot to argue heavily.

For those few hours after lunch, the world stopped. Time passed slowly. At some point I grew tired of the porch, and started wandering around the grounds, despite the heat. The grass, dried in places crunched underfoot, and the wild rose bushes were brown in spots. I wondered over all of it: to the north wall, a mile from the house. It was easily twenty feet high, the top covered with a rusting fence, spikes twisted and bent: to keep people out, or in?

And to the south of that wall, always and forever, the house. I remember how it lay, spread out beneath me: long and thin, with branching halls. A single peak stuck up from the roof— hidden to all, invisible from the ground, even from a mile away. But I saw it from my tree. It stuck up from the South Wing.

*

Just after lunch the snow was turning to ice as a cold wind blew down from the north. We ran inside, stomping our feet and shaking blown snow out of our coats. "There was a white coat here this morning. Anyone know whose it is?"

Margaret hung her coat up. "Yes. I think I saw Bernard's *friend* wearing a white coat. Maybe it's hers."

"Thanks. I saw it and got curious." I dropped my boots onto the rack. "Think we missed lunch? I'm starved."

Persephone smiled. "Bet there's something left. Mark couldn't possible eat everything."

We laughed our way to the dining room. Covered dishes waited in the middle of the table and a maid was carrying a tray of dirty dished off when we walked in. Jacqueline looked up. "Well. We're so glad you could join us. I trust your trip was successful?"

"Oh yes—we got everything we needed done. Isn't that right?" Suzanne sat down, and started lifting chicken onto her plate.

Margaret joined her. "I think I got all those small errands you had taken care of. Oh, and Jason did get that lens he needed. It is the right kind?"

I nodded, and took my turn at the chicken.

"You will show your pictures tonight, won't you?"

I looked down the table at Jacqueline. "Sure. But I do want some time to do some darkroom work. Don't forget—I've got wedding pictures, too. But they can wait."

"Oh, no. Show them too!" Suzanne said. "You

must—show them all together. Please?"

"It'll take a few days."

"We can wait. You can show them later. I would like to see the wedding at the same time."

"Me too." Persephone.

Margaret nodded.

I had a few days.

*

Miranda had an iron grip on my arm. With her other hand, she planted her cane equally firmly on the carpet, then took a step, and started over. "It's absurd really, Walk around in the snow and ice all morning, nothing. Then I get back and what do I do? First thing, I slip and sprain my ankle. Can you believe that?"

I shook my head no.

"It's really awfully good of you to help me up those stairs. I haven't trusted that banister for a while now."

I nodded again, and reached for the door, bumping the bookcase to its side. As she hobbled past me, I looked back down the hall way, the windows forcing afternoon sunlight against the wall. At the far end, in shadow, I thought I saw a form shift its weight and be still.

Miranda continued: "Did I ever tell you about the voodoo magician I saw put a curse on a man? This was years ago, in Cuba. The forties."

"What?"

"Did I ever tell you about the voodoo curse?"

"No. I don't think you did."

She stood in the doorway a moment then continued into the small anteroom. I knew the room well—bookcases to the right, flanking the window. Large drop-leaf table in the center, a desk to its left, a counter to the right, a door in the corner. I'd spent may hours in that room as a child.

She sat in a chair, below the window.

"You have time, don't you? It won't take very long."

I pulled the desk chair around and sat. The door shut behind me with a firm click, which she ignored.

"You have to remember, now, this was years ago. I was down there for something, don't remember what—all that sticks in my mind is the voodoo priest. It was a simple thing, really. By the side of the road, he drew a circle in the sand which he filled with kerosene which he then lit. Into that circle he dropped a scorpion.

"I watched him do that. It ran around the inside of the circle for a while, and discovered it was trapped. I think it must have known it couldn't get away, so it hunkered down and stung itself to death."

She reached up and turned the lamp on, filling the room with a warm orange. "Funny that, don't you think?" Miranda turned to look at me. "Have you ever known a thing to act like that?"

"Have to think about it."

She nodded and picked up her book. "Going to

do a bit of reading."

I nodded and left, pulling the door closed behind me, and I heard the key rasp in the lock, shutting me out into the house.

As I passed the shadow, there was nothing in it.

*

Inside the game room the family was gathering as I passed through. A game of hearts was gathering, and Suzanne pulled me in as I passed. "You've got to play! What kind of game'd we have without you? You're the key!" She laughed, leaning back as the cards slid out—seventeen, eighteen.

"Maybe for a hand or two."

"Knew it! Mark, you lose the bet. Jason *always* plays."

He just frowned. Then, "Very well. You win."

"What bet?"

Persephone pulled my ear close: "Suzanne bet Mark that you'd play because Mark said he thought you had better things to do with your time —"a pause "—You don't, do you?"

"No."

She smiled.

I looked down at the three cards lying in front

of me. Sorting the hand I'd gotten, I wasn't really paying much attention. I passed left, picked up what Suzanne'd given me: The Queen of Spades. A King of Diamonds, and the two of Clubs. I started the game. "I met Ogden yesterday."

"He's a NAZI." Kevin. He dropped the Ace. "Mine."

Persephone giggled. "But he isn't really German. He's a fake"

"I know. What happened to Franklin?"

"Left. Quit. Retired. Some such." Mark.

"Why?"

Kevin swept the cards up; led a low Spade. "Robert. Gave him bad pills. That's what I heard." He reached behind to the bar. "Who wants a drink?"

A chorus answered.

"Oh, yes—he had a bad heart."

Kevin nodded, handing glasses around. Ice chattered to itself. He downed his glass, refilled it. "Yes." Repeated the process.—"How bad?" Between glasses.—"Wrong dose, to strong or not right stuff. I don't know. Maybe it'd gone bad. Either, it didn't work right. Convulsions." He refilled. "Fell dead during dinner. But you know that."

I nodded. Glanced at the cards. My turn. Spades.

I dropped a card without looking, then looked. A chill grabbed me, then I realized I hadn't dropped the Queen of Spades. She still lay in my hand.

Play continued, conversation drifted. Mark accused Kevin of stacking the deck. Kevin answered by saying he'd seen Mark palming cards all evening from his pile of tricks. Katherine said she'd seen them *both* cheating . . . and we were off. I crept away in the middle, and no one noticed me leave.

Ruth and Bernard were still at their game, Ruth still winning. She smiled at me when I passed, saying good night to all. Few heard.

And as I went up, the din grew dim. My door was open a crack, golden light pouring across the hall. It was getting to be familiar. Who now?

Inside, I remembered leaving the lamp on when Suzanne dragged me out. I sat in my chair, pulling the letter from my pocket, wrinkled and dusty. It was time to find out what Uncle Robert felt was so important he had to hide it from the Family.

But as I unfolded the three white pages, my hopes plummeted: Robert and his games had struck again. The first page was a set of wavy lines that meandered all over the sheet; the second was a range of boxes, lightly colored in with blue and red pencils and the third consisted of three boxes of numbers and letters centered top to bottom on the page. Occasionally some were red instead of black.

Robert had left me a puzzle I didn't understand instead of an answer. I folded the pages back the way I'd found them, and looked around my room for a hiding place.

*

Darkness stood guard in the hallway outside my room. I went to the South Wing, to wait for the spot light, or my unknown quiet friend from the top of the stairs. I must have dozed off, propped in the darkest corner at the end of the hall. Disoriented, I tried to think of what woke me. Then the scraping sound came again, close by. A mouse ran across the floor to vanish under the third door on my left. I relaxed. Only to hear the sound again. Then the sliding noise of a rusty bold going back. Tension returned, unbidden, making my hairs stand end-wise.

At the end of the hall, a door was opening.

I tried to be quiet as I crept down the hall. The door faced me, neither of us could see each other. I don't know what I expect to find on the other side—Uncle Robert out for an evening stroll?

Some unknown fiend ready to leap forward, fangs drooling sharp claws? At that moment, just before pulling the door wide, I was glad I wasn't in a horror movie.

And I pulled, shining my light in her face.

And Margaret jumped, gasping for breath.

And I couldn't resist saying "Boo!"

She laughed. "You really scared me. What are you doing up here lurking in the dark? Jason, I'm starting to worry about what you think you're doing. Spying. Hiding in the shadows. You're not Sam Spade, you know." —a pause—"Well? I'm waiting for an explanation."

I didn't have one. At least not one she'd believe. So I said nothing: "How's the wrist?"

"Fine. Thank you . . . I still want my answer."

Looking past her into the dim room, I could see old furniture, a desk or two, boxes in piles. Some were being systematically searched—their contents in neat piles on the floor, the dust heavy with smears. "What are you looking for?" I went in.

She closed the door after me, switching on a light.

I took a good look around. As I thought, but with a new addition. Heavy cloth was thumb tacked to the bottom of the door, hiding the light.

"Who are you hiding this search from? Jacqueline? or Douglas?"

Margaret sat in a chair, looked down at the piles of papers, photos, books. "You don't miss much. Always knew you were smart. But you're surprising me. Nobody really expects you to succeed, you know."

Succeed? then I knew: *Robert.* "I'm waiting."

"Jacqueline, of course. Hiding things from Douglas is easy. He's drunk half the time and the other half he's sleeping it off."

Reaching down I grabbed the top sheet from one of the piles. The handwriting wasn't familiar—then it was. "What are you looking for in his stuff?"

"Long story."

"We've plenty of time. Better tell me all of it."

"I need a drink." Margaret opened the door. Down into the dark of the game room, where the shadows loom along the walls; some games were still in progress, their parts left out until morning. Here, after stopping, there would be no cheating until play resumed. One of many family rules.

Margaret stood at the bar, searching for some bottle. She found it, and spilled herself a glassful. Drank it down in one shot, smiled at me. "Well, I don't know where to start."

Then she collapsed, taking the bottle with her. It rolled away under the table, the sofa.

I stood a moment, unsure how to react, then ran across the snow to return dragging Ogden with me. We carried her upstairs to her room, and leaving her with Douglas and the doctor; I went to get Jacqueline up.

The whole process took maybe ten minutes.

And all hell broke without a warning.

Margaret was dead.

*

Bernice Abbot. Eugene Atget. Both photographers whose pictures show a world where the camera is an observer, not involved in the image, only recording it. Like them, I have spent years standing aside and watching—my family, my world. An observer.

Scattered images from that night —

—Douglas pacing, gesturing as if in an argument, but saying nothing, glass in hand—

—Jacqueline sitting in the room, watching Ogden go about his business—

—Persephone sitting with Josephine, both crying, a box of tissues as their feet—

—Katherine sitting in the game room, quietly playing Solitaire, glassy eyed—

—Bernard and George talking quietly—

—Ruth writing in a notebook—

—all strangely the same.

I took the bottle and hid it in a plastic bag, and went across to Dr. Ogden that morning. We had our own doctor, and when things happened, the police were rarely ever summoned. Somehow, he was expecting me, and opened the door before I could knock. "Schnell! Eingang!" He shut the door behind me just as quickly.

I held up the bag with the bottle. "I think you know what I want you to do."

He nodded. "It is gut that you brought this."

"How'd she die?"

"My facilities are poor. For certain, I can not know."

"Guess."

"Strychnine."

I followed him to his kitchen; dirtied glassware sat on the table, notes with coffee-rings under an empty mug. "This is not my specialty. I can not know for positive."

I sat in a chair. "I've got to trust someone. When was she poisoned?"

"Do not know for positive. Gut that the bottle is here brought."

"How soon?"

"If here,"—Ogden raised the bottle—"I will know."

I went back to the house, leaving him to his beakers and flasks. A few hours, and I would be back. Until then, I had some questions, and it was lunch time. The family would be gathering in the dining room for sandwiches, hot and cold. Nobody was in the mood for a full meal.

I was the last to arrive. I could feel their eyes on me at the table, setting sandwich on plate. Then follow when I sat. The room was quiet. Douglas glared at me from across the room, as if wanting me to shrivel up and die, too.

The radiator whirred in the background, and the wind blew snow against a window. Quiet.

Jacqueline spoke: "Jason, why don't you tell us what happened?"

The family looked at me, expectant.

Then, "Yes, Jason, why don't you tell us all exactly what happened, hmmm?" Douglas crossed to stand over my chair.

"We're all waiting, Jason. Tell us all how you killed my wife."

More quiet.

"Strychnine."

Douglas downed his drink and retreated to the sideboard. Someone shifted in their chair. A fork clicked on a plate. Quiet, again.

"She was poisoned, just as Robert was. Aunt Margaret was murdered because someone—one of the family—thought she knew why Robert died. She may have, but she died before I could find out, so I'm as much in the dark as anybody.

"But the murderer that is."

Katherine seemed to smile at that. I had time to wonder why before Jacqueline said, "I think we should talk in private. Leave us."

They left, taking their plates with them.

Jacqueline set hers on the table and crossed to check the hall. She stayed by the big sliding oak doors. I turned back to my sandwich.

"Why did Robert come back?"

"I'm asking the questions. You will answer. Understood?"

I nodded.

"Good." —a pause—"Margaret didn't find what she's looking for. I already know that. Margaret isn't my interest. Tell me about the . . . coffin."

"Not much to tell. Pulled out by three people, probably men, opened and the body taken."

"Have you found them, yet? I know you've been looking."

"No."

"Why?"

"Their boots aren't in the house. None of the boots here match the notching."

"Then I suggest you try again. Look harder. I don't like mysteries."

She checked the hall again.

"Who do you expect?" I said.

"Don't know. That's the problem."

"Oh." I set my empty plate on the floor. "How much do you know about Ruth?"

"Bernard's pet? Not a very bright girl."

I nodded, deciding to keep my worries to myself for the moment. "What about this deal with Samuel?"

"I know of no deal."

Again, she looked out the door. I walked over to look out the window. "Why did Robert leave?"

"That's not important, and it's no concern of yours. If you needed to know, then I might consider telling you. You don't."

I turned back from the window, wanting to argue, but Jacqueline was gone, the door open. Interview at an end.

*

The maid was emptying the trash when I got back to my room. The servants came in and went out on their own schedule. They all lived in town, working here, but never remaining for too long. But privacy did have its limits. She looked up startled, "Excuse me, sir, I'll be out of your way in a moment." And headed for the door.

"Hold it. Joan isn't it?" —she nodded—"You know most everything in these rooms, don't you?"

Joan shifted and looked toward the door.

"Don't worry. I thought you might. Tell me, does anyone keep any bottles—they don't have to be big ones—in their rooms?"

"Sir, I don't understand. Wine?"

"No. Joan, why don't you have a seat?" I went over and checked the hall. Empty, Quiet. "I need you to do something for me. I want you—"

She looked like she might run into the hall.

"Relax. I want you to keep you eyes open for a small bottle—any small bottle—that looks like it might have poison in it. When you find it. And you will. Leave it alone, but come and tell me immediately." I checked the hall, no change. "If you can't find me come in here and leave a note"—I looked around for a place, discarding ideas quickly—"Leave it inside the bureau. When you pull out a drawer, there is a space underneath. Leave it there."

"Ok?"

She nodded, hurrying out the door, only looking back to give me a funny look. As if to say you're a crazy one, aren't you? I smiled to myself as the door swung shut in a draft. Perhaps.

*

There have been changes. When threatened, the Family, whether consciously or unconsciously, closes ranks against any threat. I am the outsider, the threat. Now the games are closed to me and when I pass silence falls. Many pairs of eyes watch as I go by on my way to the library, the note in my pocket stiff and cold as the grave.

At the door, I paused. Afternoon light cut a swatch of floor down the hall, dark tile reflecting back in wine black red. The door swung open and I stepped into the bright afternoon gale. Silence rained down hard on my ears, my footsteps lost in the rug as I crossed to Jacqueline's chair, by the Mercury statue. "I got your note."

"Obviously, or else you wouldn't be here."

I nodded and sat.

"Jason. You always were such a smart little boy. But I wonder: just how smart are you, now?

I know you've been avoiding the issue of your photographs. You brought the case, as I specified —" She turned toward me from looking out the window "—Ah, I see you have. Give them to me."

I passed over my portfolio case. "These are the prints. I wasn't sure—didn't bring the slides. You can't really see them without a projector."

She took it and nodding, unzipped the black case. It took almost a half hour, and the clock was just starting to chime for the second time when Jacqueline finished. She had said nothing, her face unreadable while she looked. Handing it back, "You have no reason to be ashamed of your work. Show it to Miranda; she will be interested."

Relieved, I took my portfolio back. "Thanks. I will."

I started to go, but she stopped me: "A moment. I know Margaret was searching through Roberts things the night she died."

I sat down again. "Yes."

"Find out what she was looking for. And who killed her; I believe you are right and who ever killed Robert also killed Margaret. And for the same reason. Find that for me."

"I've got a problem—I. Nevermind, I'll sort it out myself."

"Good. Now then, why don't you start with

me?"

I sat the portfolio on the table, and leaned back. The afternoon sun was fading, changing the room from bright to dim. "Alright." I turned on a lamp. "Let's begin.

"Last night, when Margaret died. Where were you?"

"In my room, asleep."

"Did you hear anyone moving around—I know you sleep lightly."

"No, but do remember that I am on a floor by myself. I heard nothing until after. . . ."

I leaned forward. "On a different tack, what do you know about Ruth?"

"She came with Bernard." Jacqueline smiled and leaned back into the winged chair. "She was an 'assistant' of some sort in his business. I have no idea what it is this month, however. He and Samuel have something going on right now. I don't know what."

"If I can think of anything else to ask you, I'll come by later on. Thanks." I went to the door. "Oh yes—could you tell people to cooperate with me? It is such a nuisance—"

"No. That is not in my power to do."

I felt the door click shut behind me, and I was alone in the hall. I started back to my room, but then stopped and went back—I had forgotten my portfolio.

The library door was locked. I pressed my ear against it, but could hear nothing more than my blood pounding in my ears.

*

Snow covered all the floor: drifts in the corners, flows across the entire floor. White, quite an inappropriate color for a funeral—black figures stood out in high contrast to it, their breaths gray against the dark walls.

I watched from the background, present but not welcome. On my way out, I had feared a second outburst from Douglas, but he just walked sullenly along beside Margaret's coffin, his nose bright red in a pale face turned towards the winds.

There is little that I remember from what was said. The usual things—loving mother, good wife, kind woman—ashes to dust, etc.

Inside it was dark, outside the full bright of noon bore down on fresh snow. I went out into the day, remembering Robert's coffin lying in the shaft of light. Our footprints stretched a dark band back through the woods, to the garden of coffins and into the house.

It was on my way back that I saw the footprint.

Perhaps it was precisely because I was so busy looking down at the black of the path, streaked with shuffled snow that I saw it.

The notching was familiar.

Bending down, I pulled off my glove, and felt around for the sketch I'd made, and it matched.

They led off into the woods. I followed. The trees stood silently watchful as I passed beneath them. A black squirrel watched me as I passed, before running across the snow and up. Scratching sounds drifted down.

The house was to my left as I stepped out of the woods, the trail running beneath my feet. Dr. Ogden's house stood to my right. The footprints led there.

Now, why, I thought, *would Ol' Ogden be corpse snatching?* I ran the rest of the way to his door, confident that he would be at the funeral for a while yet. [There was nothing I could do about him knowing I'd followed his trail. My feet left prints as good as his.]

I reached the door, feeling winded and panting freezing breaths, making my lungs sore. Looking back, it was as still as before I passed. The black squirrel jumped from one tree to another, making the branches wave. All clear.

As expected, the door was not locked.

I went in, tracking snow with me. Warmth welcomed me. A radiator in one of the rooms hissed quietly. Silence.

Unbuttoning my coat, but keeping my gloves on—why I've no idea—I went to the door he'd so carefully closed for my previous visits. Jacqueline would say I was harassing the staff.

I looked around before going in.

Inside, it was a fastidious sort of messiness: a scarred roll-top desk to the left of the door, the photograph to the right. A worn oval rug in the middle of the room, a bookcase opposite. A swivel chair with an orange corduroy cushion sat in the middle, bare bulb hanging over it all. Books with sheets of paper stuck in them sat in piles, or half open on the floor. Vinyl records lay in groups against the walls, beside the bookcase. The window looked out over frost and the courtyard. Ballpoint pins were scattered about, and a manuscript lay next to the typewriter, on the desk.

Sitting in his chair, I could see the courtyard, and look at what was on the desk. Turning from the still empty courtyard, I looked at the manuscript, but it turned out to be just a pile of blank pages.

The center drawer wasn't much more

interesting, either: paperclip chains, a novel in German whose contents I guessed from the cover. To the right, a box of cigars, and a stapler. To the left, a box of *Oreo* cookies, resting on some envelopes.

Cookie stuck in my mouth, I pulled them out.

They were empty.

I was starting to wonder if perhaps Jacqueline would be right in saying I was harassing the staff.

In the middle of the second cookie I realized they were stale. Leaning back in the chair, I watched the squirrel run across the courtyard, and start digging at a flower bed.

On the premise that nobody could keep such an orderly desk without being psychotic, I turned back to it. When I got to the cigar box I realized there was no ashtray in the office.

Lifting it out, it was rather heavy, and something rattled. Turning around, I dumped it out onto the floor. A handful of cigars fell out, then nothing. Just enough to cover the top of a long piece of board that was glued into the top of the box: it had a false bottom.

That's when Ogden came in.

Or, at least I expected him to. If I lived in a cheap detective novel, he would certainly come in the moment I turned my back on the window;

however, he did not.

Several minutes and some searching later, I found that Ogden is one of the many people who do not own sharp letter openers. So, I went into the kitchen, dropping the box on the table, next to a German novel with a lurid cover, to get a knife. Eventually, I had to use a scalpel from the small examination room. All his knives would have given warm butter a run for its money.

After all that work, I was disappointed: expecting a gun or gold coins, anything but what I found. Inside, a key wrapped in a silk embroidered handkerchief with a blue rose on it.

Pulling the key to my room out of my pocket, I held it up for comparison: it wouldn't fit my door, but there was something familiar about it—the style of the turned metal of the eye where it would join a ring. It fit a door somewhere in the house, but I didn't know where.

Realizing how much time I'd spent on the box, I grabbed the cigars and dropped them back into the box. I shut the drawer, and headed for the door, pushing the key down into my pant pocket.

*

I was just pulling the door open when I heard voices. Looking back through the trees, dark people came forward, their words indistinct, distant. Pulling it open, I went into the mud room. Ruth stood by the inner door, hanging her coat up.

Turning toward me, she smiled distantly, then sat, pulling her boots off. "Shut the door, will you? It's cold."

I did, and unbuttoned my coat, reaching for a hanger. "You have a white coat."

"Last time I checked."

Nodding, I sat opposite her, shivering when the door opened—Mark and Kevin came in, laughing at some joke. "Left early to get away from Douglas? Smart man!" Mark dropped into the seat next to me.

He unbuttoned his coat, but didn't get up to hang it. I looked over at him, questioning: *What?*

"Why don't you come and see my paintings. Then, perhaps, you'll be more . . . able to help me talking to Miranda."

"What 'to Miranda?'" She said, stepping in.

"Nothing. Think about it, okay?" Mark hung his coat, then went into the house still wearing his boots.

"It's those pictures, I'll bet."

I nodded; looked up, and caught Ruth smiling at me. Miranda stepped forward, putting her coat on a hook, no hanger. I reached under my chair, feeling for my shoes.

"See you 'round." Ruth left.

Kevin grunted and followed her.

"Odd, isn't it?" Carefully bending down, Miranda lifted her shoes onto the chair next to her.

"What's odd?"

Pulling them on, she stood. "If you've not noticed, I'll not be saying."

And then I was alone. Notice what?

*

The key was an unwelcome extra weight in my pocket, so I went off to find a place to stick it until I could find out which door it matched. My room was out, obviously—it would be the first place a searcher would go, and I had the feeling that it wouldn't be the first time.

In the course of my wanderings, I ended up in Mark's "studio"—a small room on the third floor, close and warm. I looked around—Mark kept a neat studio: an easel stood in one corner, a canvas in place, a dropcloth spread over the bare wood floor. A cardboard box with CORN FLAKES in big red letters stood in the corner, painted canvases stuck in it. A folding chair leaned against the wall, and a little table with paint tubes arranged neatly on it, a glass filled with brushes on the floor next to it. The only thing out of place was the coffee cup in the corner.

I went to the window and looked out, the white roof blinding me for a moment, then I could see the fine line that separated it from the ground. Black trees reached up towards me, the gray sky.

Turning back, I rubbed my eyes. The room was suddenly dimly red-yellow. A minute later I could see again. Crossing to the box, I pulled out the first canvas.

I looked at it for a while, and I knew why Miranda didn't want to show his work.

*

I went back downstairs to the second floor, and walked back to my room. The door was shut, and a note folded in half stuck into it. Pulling it down, I read it and went downstairs to collect the package that had arrived for me.

The foyer was cold, and some sprinkles of snow floated in the middle of small puddles of water on the white marble floor. The box sat by the door, and I knew what was in it, and was happy it'd arrived.

Stooping to pick it up, I heard a low whistle from behind me.

Ruth stood in the doorway, smiling at me. "Need a hand?"

"Not really, but I'd welcome the company. Everybody seems to have disappeared this afternoon."

"I know. Been wandering the halls myself."

I nodded, and bent back to the box.

"Here let me help you." Ruth took the other side of the box, and lifted it along with me. "Got it?"

"Thanks, yes."

"What's in it?"

"Come on, you can help me unpack."

We walked down the hall, and across from the study Ruth opened the door for me. The room was a mirror image of the study—a two-story high ceiling, a fireplace stretching from the floor to the top, large enough to walk into. A Christmas tree sat in the center of the room, sofas and chairs pulled back, sparkling ornaments arranged around it, presents beneath.

"When did the tree go up?"

Ruth turned the lights on, filling the room with gaudy sparkles that danced over everything.

"Just before we went down for the wedding."

"Oh." I set the box on the floor. "Hand me the letter opener on that side table, would you? Thanks." I cut the tape open, and pulled the flaps apart.

White foam peanuts drifted out.

"I know what those are—Christmas presents!"

I smiled, nodded. The key I got at Ogden's dug into my leg, and I shifted to stop the sharp pain it made. Examination of the key reveals three things, not all of them immediately obvious. First, it is from the house, one of the old keys molded into an ornate object, with a low-relief vine wrapping itself around the entire shaft. The loop at the end where it attached to a ring is a spiral in that vine. In this regard, there is no difference between it and the rest of the interior door keys. Second, it has not been used to open any door in a long while— that is clear from the lack of any recent scratches or marks on the shaft from where it would meet the door plate. Third, the key is made from brass, while the other keys are made from steel.

Ruth knelt opposite me and scooped some of the foam out, onto the floor, then reached back in for the red-wrapped box within.

"Are they all here?"

"No, only about half, the rest are still upstairs

in my room. I just couldn't carry all of 'em in my luggage."

"I've always loved presents. Like to shake them and guess what's inside. You ever do that?"

Laughing, "No, not really."

"You're kidding—you never wondered what people are hiding, waiting to spring on someone else?"

I laughed, "Not with presents, no."

*

Dinner was later than usual. Gradually, the rest of the family came wondering in, until everyone had arrived, and the clock on the mantle chimed nine. Miranda was the last to arrive, walking with difficulty, leaning on an old cane as she headed for her chair.

I had arrived early, and watched as the glasses, then plates and silverware were laid out on the white linen of the table. The two servants moved quietly, softly speaking a word or two, as they went about their business. I sat in my chair, a pile of contact sheets lying on the seat next to me.

The wedding pictures looked good: not too much grain, dramatic where appropriate.

Leaning into the light, I pushed the loupe against the paper, Frame 14 beneath it. A general shot of the family greeted my eye—virtually a family portrait, but I didn't remember taking it. Anna stood beside Pauline, smiling at her new son-in-law. Behind them, Bernard stood frowning at Suzanne who was gesturing with her champagne flute, while Mark crossed to where they were. Miranda sat at a table with Jacqueline who was staring across at Katherine, who stood at the back talking at a man in a black suit with a white scarf draped across his neck—I didn't remember seeing *him* before.

Shifting, I reached back to the pile I'd been marking on for the group shot of the entire family. Bending over it, I searched for the black suit, the white scarf. I moved from face to face, looking closely, but did not find him.

I turned back to the other image, this time to look more closely at the man who stood slightly behind Suzanne, slightly stooped forward, face partially obscured.

I couldn't tell who he was. Frowning I moved to the next picture, but it was a different part of the room, and he wasn't in it any longer.

Circling frame 14 with my grease pencil and making a mental note to enlarge it first, I looked up to see Mark standing across the table from me.

"Hi. Can you come up after dinner and take

a look at my paintings? I remember you saying that you needed to see them before talking to Miranda."

"Sure, but I don't know that she'll listen to me any more than you."

Mark sat down. "She will. You're the one she likes best—you say 'take Marks work,' she'll do it." He reached across and pulled the contact page across. "Wedding pictures? They look good— when're you going to enlarge?" —I nodded— "enlarge them?"

"Maybe tonight, or in the morning."

He nodded, looking back over his shoulder to Kevin who had just walked in. "His wedding pictures, want to see?"

Nodding, Kevin took the sheet. "What's the mark for?"

"So I can find the negative more easily."

Nodding, He handed it back. "Look good. Can I see the photos when you've got them?"

I nodded, leaning back into my chair, thoughts drifting back to what was happening around me. Douglas sat at the foot of the table, opposite Jacqueline, Miranda on her right. Margaret's chair was conspicuously empty.

"Pass the salt, please?" Katherine said to me for the second time.

"Oh, sorry—here it is."

"Thanks."

"You're welcome."

"Jason's going to have his wedding pictures ready in a day or two." Mark smiled, leaning forward, "I got to see his proofs before dinner and they look really good—impressive."

"Thanks."

"You'll have to give us a proper showing," Anna said, "But I'd be happy with just looking at the proofs? Could I see them later?"

"Yes, you will." Jacqueline smiled.

I said yes to Anna, and turned to Jacqueline, "I left my portfolio somewhere—was it in the library. I've looked around and I think that's got to be the place. Did you see it?"

"I meant to tell you—you left it on the table there."

"Thanks. I was a little concerned that someone might have moved it." I set my fork down and reached for my glass. "I thought I saw someone in the house this afternoon sneaking around, like they didn't want to be seen."

Suzanne laughed. "That was our game! You know, hide and seek?"

"This was before it."

"Oh."

"Why don't you just shut up you"

Jacqueline cut him off: "Douglas, you're drunk."

I heard someone say, softly, "always," the voice was feminine. But before I could look around to see who it was, Douglas was standing.

He dropped his glass on the floor, and leaned against the table heavily; a glass fell over, the wine running blood red across the table. "Now listen here you bitch. I'm tired of your running people into the ground. You're a bitch who should be put in her place."

He started around the table, and fell as he passed Bernard, with a loud crash. The stream of wine reached the edge of the table and started dripping onto the marble floor.

Bernard stood up, pulling Douglas to his feet. "Now, that's enough of that talk. You're going upstairs and sleep it off." Douglas struggled against Bernard, trying to hit him. Kevin grabbed his feet, and the two carried Douglas, now quieted, out.

Someone thought to put their napkin into the lake of wine, and the dripping slowed to a stop. It left a stain and I could only think of blood as it dripped off the edge, splattering on the floor as everyone jumped away.

*

Mercury looked off, into the distance, his hand raised to shade his eyes, his foot resting on a zephyr, my portfolio resting in front of the statue, on the table. I stood, my hand on the case, eyes looking out into the dark of night. Faint moonlight filtered down through the black trees, the branched dark against dark sky.

A soft wind blew a sheet of snow across the hidden patio. Behind that loomed the dark coffins of statues. I could feel Mark's eyes on me. "Be with you in a minute."

"Some scene."

I nodded; he continued. "Wonder what really set him off."

Waiting, I watched a second sheet of snow drift across.

"Another storm is rising."

Mark crossed heavily, his feet thumping against the floor. He stopped just behind me, and to the left.

Silence.

The sound of a breeze whispering ragged around the corner of the house, the scrape of snow against glass.

"Why do you want to sell your work so badly?"

"What?"

"Why do you want to sell your work so badly? There are lots of galleries besides Miranda's in the world."

He shifted from his right to his left; I watched him without turning.

"New artists seldom have many sales for the first couple of shows."

He stood a moment longer, then turned and left, saying, "Talk to her," over his shoulder. I stood looking out the window for a moment, then I left, the Mercury statue casting a faint shadow on the dark wood.

*

I was surprised to find Anna in the game room, a pad of paper on her knee, pen in hand, eyes focused of some point a thousand miles away. Normally, she spent her time at a desk off in her study, working quietly on her writings.

She looked up abruptly as I past. "Jason, I've been wanting to see those pictures you took— you know, the wedding? Could I see them now, please?"

"Sure." I smiled and handed her the pile of proofs. "The ones with the blue 'X' I'm going to print." —I handed her the china marker—"Mark any that you want with a star, that way I won't get them confused." I shifted from squatting to sitting on the floor.

Bernard and Ruth were playing chess, again. *She must be cold,* I thought, looking at the short dress, her long legs. "Who's winning?"

Ruth looked around Bernard. "I am."

He shifted uncomfortably. "She told me she wasn't very good. I think she was lying."

Ruth laughed; I smiled.

Anna tapped me on the shoulder. I turned back to her.

"Can you make me an extra copy of this one"—she pointed to a frame—"Pauline would just love to have it framed, I'm sure."

"Happy to. Um . . . put two stars on that one, so I'll know to make three copies."

"Ok." I watched her hand move. "These are really good. I'm glad someone took pictures besides that awful man. He spent most of his time drinking the champagne. Is there some reason that wedding photographers are always fat?"

I laughed. "Not that I know of."

Anna smiled, moving to the next page. As she did so, the pile squirted out of her grip, leaving her holding two pages—the top and bottom. "Oh, now what have a gone and done? I hope they're not out of order."

"Don't worry—they weren't in any order to start with."

Suzanne came in and bent to help with the jumble of proofs. "Can I look too?"

I shrugged.

"Goody."

Squaring the pages back into a pile, Anna continued looking, passing them to Suzanne when she finished. "Who's that?"

I stood up, to get a better look. Anna's think finger pointed to the man in frame 14. "I don't know. I thought you might—or maybe he was invited by Jack's family."

"We didn't invite him."

"Let me see." Suzanne stood on the other side of the chair. "Who?"

Anna pointed, again.

"Who's he?"

"That's what we were wondering."

"Is he in any other —"

"No. I saw him just before dinner, forgot all about it until just now. No—I didn't see him in any others, including the group shot."

Suzanne giggled. "*It's a conspiracy!* We should ask Katherine about tall, dark strangers."

"I'll ask her." Anna handed back the contact sheets. "Thanks, Jason. Let's finish this later.

Either of you know where Katherine went?"

We shook our heads no.

Anna sighed, and headed for the stairs. It was only later that I realized she'd gone up, into the South Wing.

*

I lay back into my chair, hand lying on the edge of the desk, fingers absently turning the key. The yellow Bakelite clock on corner of the desk said it was late, but not quite late enough.

There was a creak outside my door.

Fingers frozen for a moment, then I stuck the key into my pocket, softly crossing to the door. Knowing that it wasn't quite shut, I grabbed the knob and pulled it open.

Darkness hung in the hall. Stepping out into it, I looked right, then left; saw nothing but empty darkness, lit slightly by the bank of windows. The shadows hid unknown depths.

A banshee flew howling along the wall, rattling the window panes, and filling the hallway with the seething scrape of snow. The light seethed, swirling with the same swirling patterns of rings and spirals within spirals, as on a hot day, but it was cold, and night.

I was alone and it was almost time.

*

The heat rose in long thin plumes, making each flagstone appear a pool of hot, invisible water that evaporated as you approached. The air, too, moved in long, thin columns, leaving the ground still, but the trees above rustling softly. The statues stood each looking out at its appointed part. Here, Mars, there, Aphrodite each gazing distantly at the other, across the breadth of the courtyard.

The leaf-shadows sat heavily on the ground.

"Check."

I turned from my gazing into the courtyard to survey the board. The knight threatened my king, but I could take it with a pawn.

I turned back from the window: "Check."

Miranda smiled.

I moved my king; the game was going badly for me.

"Mate."

I nodded, looking at the board: I had seen it coming, but could not avoid it. Perhaps I should have conceded earlier.

"Another?"

We turned the board around. This time I was red. We set the pieces onto their squares—red queen on the red square—and began again.

"You shouldn't let someone else take control

when the first move is yours. That's why you lost." She smiled, and drank her iced tea. "It's better to act only when your position is first protected. Then you have a defense ready."

"So, I should proceed only when my next move has been set up by my last."

"Yes. Otherwise you're just a pawn."

I nodded. "And this is true outside of chess."

Miranda smiled; I understood.

*

Winter —

Images of ice and cold, snow and dark trees, their leafless limbs black cracks against a smooth gray sky. The light is bluish as it glides in through the windows to cut hard shadows on the furniture. Mercury stands waiting at the window, forever looking out across the flanks of upright boxes, each a narrow house for the statue within.

—My memory flew through the study, and the harsh cold light of day, to return to my room in the darker black of night. I looked at the yellow clock and knew the house would be asleep, but not at rest.

It was time.

On my way out, I pulled my door shut behind me and locked it, putting my key away. The other key, Ogden's key, rested sharply in my pocket.

I headed for the South Wing quietly, pausing often to listen for the footsteps, the creak that would tell of another, waiting, moving as silently as I, watchful.

The windows continued to fill the hallway with seething light, the scrape-scrape of snow on glass. I stood to the side, in shadow, watching the emptiness back to my room, then turning to the other doors, each with its bar of night across the sill.

I went down the stairs, stopping to listen at the landing between floors, the gilt framed mirror reflecting back darkly. The corner table held a dried flower arrangement, flanked by an ornate green lamp.

Normally ignored, they had a still-life quality about them; I tucked them away in the back of my mind to photograph later, then went down into the game room.

And I was not alone. "You have not seen me; I am not here." The man said, as he shifted his weight in the dark corner of the room. The hall light was on behind me, but he had moved his chair so it sat out of sight to that light.

"Right." I knew the voice—I only had to remember whose. Then I did: "Why aren't you here, Uncle Samuel?"

He leaned forward. He'd grown a beard since I'd last seen him, but the blue eyes, the salt and pepper gray in his hair were unmistakable. It was Samuel. "You ask too many questions."

I sat down on a chair beside the chess table. Bernard and Ruth's game had been left for the night. Red was beating black. "If you want me to keep quiet, you'd better explain why."

"This is blackmail."

I nodded—*yes, it was.*

"Fine." He leaned back into the chair. "If I officially return for Christmas, I think I'll be killed."

"Like Margaret."

"Or blamed. I arrived during the funeral this morning. How'd it happen?"

"Strychnine. She drank it. Someone put it in the liquor."

Samuel nodded, back in the shadows. In the distance a floorboard creaked. The sound of blowing snow drifted down to us. There was someone else in hallway, listening. He stood and walked over to the sidebar, lifting the bottles to inspect them. "Has anyone checked the rest of these?"

"No." I walked over, "It was hard enough to

find out what Margaret drank, if you want to be safe, just don't drink anything."

He nodded, and walked over to the chess game. "What do you know about Ruth?"

I turned to follow. "Not much. She arrived with Bernard for the wedding. I haven't seen her before." I stopped by the board. "She is good at chess. I don't think Bernard has beaten her yet." The game had ended, pieces were scattered around the board, their roles over.

Samuel nodded.

"What do you know?"

It was time for bed. "Not much more than you do." He turned toward the stairs, going up the way I came down. "I have things to do. Good night." He turned and went up with silent footsteps. A moment later I heard the soft click of a cane on wood. Frowning, I watched him go. There weren't going to be any more answers. I followed after him, and all at once I understood. There was no mystery to solve. I was just the red herring, a distraction while Miranda got her revenge.

Michael Betancourt is an artist, theorist and historian. His movies have screened internationally at the Black Maria Film Festival, Art Basel Miami Beach, Contemporary Art Ruhr, Athens Video Art Festival, Syros International Film Festival, Festival des Cinemas Differents de Paris, Anthology Film Archives, Millennium Film Workshop, the San Francisco Cinematheque's Crossroads, and Experiments in Cinema among others. His writing complements his movie making and has been translated into Chinese, French, German, Greek, Italian, Japanese, Persian, Portuguese, and Spanish, and published in many magazines, including *The Atlantic, Make Magazine, Millennium Film Journal, Leonardo, Semiotica,* and *CTheory.* He wrote *The _____ Manifesto,* and the books *The Critique of Digital Capitalism, Glitch Art in Theory and Practice,* and *Beyond Spatial Montage: Windowing.*